THE
FALCONER

Alice Thompson

TWO RAVENS
PRESS

Published by Two Ravens Press Ltd.
Green Willow Croft
Rhiroy
Lochbroom
Ullapool
Ross-shire IV23 2SF

www.tworavenspress.com

The right of Alice Thompson to be identified as author of this work has been asserted by her in accordance with the Copyright, Designs and Patent Act, 1988. © Alice Thompson, 2008.

ISBN: 978-1-906120-23-8

British Library Cataloguing in Publication Data: a CIP record for this book can be obtained from the British Library.

Designed and typeset in Sabon by Two Ravens Press.

Cover Illustration: *Les Eaux Profondes* 1941 by René Magritte, Private Collection, courtesy of Fondation Magritte and The Menil Collection © ADAGP, Paris and DACS, London 2008

Printed on Forest Stewardship Council-certified paper by Antony Rowe Ltd, Chippenham, UK.

About the Author

The Falconer is critically-acclaimed author Alice Thompson's fourth novel. The former keyboard player with post-punk eighties band, The Woodentops, was joint winner with Graham Swift of the James Tait Black Memorial Prize for fiction for her first novel, *Justine*. Her second novel, *Pandora's Box*, was shortlisted for The Stakis Prize for Scottish Writer of the Year. Alice is also a past winner of a Creative Scotland Award. She lives in Edinburgh.

Previous Novels:

Justine
Pandora's Box
Pharos

For more information about the author, see
www.tworavenspress.com

To A.D.T. and M.A.

Thank you

Full fathom five thy father lies
Of his bones are coral made
Those are pearls that were his eyes.
Nothing of him that doth fade,
But doth suffer a sea-change
Into something rich and strange.

The Tempest

Chapter 1

The long train journey began to take on the form of a monotonous dream. However, the landscape continued to mutate outside beyond the window. Cities turned to grass and then fields rose up in the shape of mountains. Light was fading in the carriage where the solitary passenger was sitting but she didn't notice the shadows falling over her. Iris Tennant was going where she would find space and solitude. She would be leaving behind the city full of strangers.

One by one, the gas lamps of the remote cottages outside were being lit. These cottages looked self-contained, so enticing out there in the dusk. She wanted the train to stop for her so that she could get off and walk across the fields to one of them. To disappear into one of those little glowing homes with low slung roofs and rough patches of field sloping down to the river.

From outside her door, the train guard switched on the compartment light. Iris turned from the window and pulled out a novel from her handbag. She had just completed the first page when there was a sudden screeching of brakes. The train was approaching the next station. It came to a stop, billows of steam obscuring her view of the platform. A few moments later the whistle blew and the train started up again, juddering so much that the words of her book began to dance about on the page. As she tried to focus on the print, she became aware that a man had entered her carriage.

The passenger stopped just inside the carriage door and removed his trilby to reveal a finely drawn face with guarded eyes. He seemed slightly abstract, as if his face was an idealized version of a more primitive self. The tailoring of his pale suit had an understated finish. He lifted up a suitcase onto the overhanging shelf – the tan leather lid was smattered with peeling labels – and sat down on the wooden seat diagonally across from her. Iris wondered what this well-dressed man was doing in the third-class compartment.

She returned to her novel, but she became conscious that the stranger was staring at her. She looked up and met his eyes: they looked at her levelly. The irises were a very pale grey, like mist.

'Forgive me,' he said softly, 'I saw you as I walked past your compartment. I had to come in.'

He spoke perfectly enunciated English – too perfect, she thought; she could hear the faint trace of a German accent.

'Haven't we met before?' he asked.

'I'm afraid you must be mistaken,' she replied, keeping her voice flat. A tie-pin in the shape of an eagle glinted between the lapels of his suit.

Outside, the landscape was growing ever more desolate. The darkness of the wide-open countryside stretched out into the dusk for miles. The train rumbled on as if under its own momentum and she felt as if they were now flying, like witches, through the night air. The light of the train was throwing a peculiar glow on the man, making him appear more exact.

'Now I look at you more closely, it's obvious you are not her,' he said. 'The likeness has gone. I'm sorry; it must have been the odd light.'

A few moments later he stood up, took his suitcase down from the shelf and left the carriage. She crossed her bare legs. She could feel the line of sweat being drawn between her thighs, damp and hot. She looked down at her unpainted toes peeping out from between the soft, red-kid leather of her sandals. The faint trace of her lavender perfume was merging with the oily smell of the train.

The train gently swayed from side to side, as if trying to rock her to sleep. Suddenly it went pitch-black outside – the train had gone into a tunnel and the loudness of the roaring train was deafening. The light in the carriage now seemed insanely bright, the brash luminosity of an asylum.

Her reflection in the window was thrown into heightened relief. Iris saw her dark eyes looking back with their usual air of objectivity, her lips fixed in an unforgiving line. There was no aura of emotion in her long, indifferent face. Her face was in stasis; it was like looking at a portrait of someone who had died years ago. But then, just for a moment, the eyes became paler, more expressive, the nose narrower and shorter, the mouth more sensual; her sister's face looked back at her, the backdrop of the reflected train carriage behind her.

And Iris felt for a certain moment that a parallel train was running beside her in the tunnel with Daphne sitting inside it. Daphne was giving Iris her direct, vivacious look with just the flicker of a smile at her lips, as definite and tinily specific as the quiver of a bird's wing.

Alighting at her destination, Iris was surprised to see the man in the trilby get off the train, a few carriages down. A Bentley was waiting for him, which drove off into the darkness.

Iris stayed that night in the nearest village inn, and at noon the following day a hired car with a shaky undercarriage dropped her off at the bottom of Glen Almain. It was a hot day in early August, with the kind of heat that seemed to make the pale blue petals of the harebells tremble. The only signs of life were the flies hovering in the still air.

Carrying her suitcase, she began to walk up the glen's road. She passed an old school-house, and noticed a small boy staring at her through the window. He was unnaturally pale, with hair as white as the seeds of a dandelion clock. Two dead falcons were pinned to the front door.

Almain Lodge house stood at the far end of the glen where the road turned into an avenue of trees. The lodge-house was situated almost at the foot of the mountains, and its roof and two large chimneys were visible just above the branches of surrounding fir trees. It had a small, well-kept garden of lawn and rhododendrons.

A woman stood at the door like the little wooden figure of a weather-house – out, because of the sun. She swept back her dark hair from her small, rosy-cheeked face with a calloused hand.

'Miss Drummond, is it?'

Iris nodded.

'I'm the housekeeper, Mrs. Elliot. I'm to take you up to the castle.'

The two women walked up the straight avenue, lined by huge beech trees whose heavy silver limbs reached out over their heads. A small loch lay to one side where the field dipped down, a rough causeway of stones leading to an isle at the centre of the loch. They walked for ten minutes along the avenue before reaching a huge cliff of red rock. The avenue turned sharply right into a cobblestoned courtyard. Veering up in front of them was a huge nineteenth-century castle made of red stone. Ornately turreted, the castle's small paned windows looked feeble in the thick walls of red sandstone. They gave the baronial castle a secret, introverted look.

Down below the courtyard, towards the mountains, stretched the most beautiful formal gardens Iris had ever seen. Borders which ran along each terrace were filled with blocks of azure blue. Dahlias and hollyhocks of pink and white added a careful incoherence. Pale lemon roses, royal purple lavender and low box-hedges, laid out in different shapes, formed interweaving patterns. Ancient yew trees crouched along the edge of the lawns. Stone statues of men and women, mottled by age, stood elegantly positioned about the gardens as if in a petrified dance.

Suddenly there was a piercing shriek. Iris heard the rustle of wings and a tall, shining peacock strutted by her feet across the courtyard, dragging its train of feathers. It fanned out its tail in a brilliant display of emerald finery.

'Miss Drummond? We're waiting for you!' called Mrs Elliot, who was lingering impatiently for her at the main door to the castle. Iris ran up to join her and followed her into the cold entrance hall. The darkness after the bright light of the gardens momentarily blinded her. As Iris adjusted to the gloom she could make out shields of faded heraldry hanging on the walls. The bare flagstones gave off a sweet and dusty smell. For a moment, Iris wondered what on earth she was doing here.

'Lord Melfort had to leave suddenly on urgent business last night, for the Western Isles. It will be Lady Melfort who will see you tomorrow morning,' Mrs Elliot said, and disappeared down the shadowy corridor as a girl not much older than fourteen, but with an overworked, whippet's face, took Iris' suitcase.

The housemaid led Iris up the servants' stairs to an unassuming room on the first floor. An oak bed covered in a thick patchwork quilt lay next to a simple table and armchair. A chest of drawers stood in the corner and a threadbare rug covered the floor. That evening, as Iris prepared for bed, she wondered in which of the castle's rooms Daphne had slept and what had been her dreams.

Chapter 2

The table had been set when Iris came down to breakfast the next morning. A bowl of blowsy red roses filled a vase on the sideboard, and the breakfast was set out in silver platters below. She opened the lids to reveal creamy scrambled eggs, kippers shiny with butter and slices of hot toast. She was the first one down to breakfast and for a while she ate cautiously, in silence. She heard male voices outside in the hall and the sound of laughter and her heart beat slightly faster, but no-one else came in, and she heard the castle door shut behind them as they went outside.

A few minutes later a girl of about fifteen, wearing trousers and an open-necked white shirt, skipped into the room, helped herself to some toast and then turned round to see Iris for the first time. In the morning light she reminded Iris – with her wide open eyes, small mouth and triangular face – of a sylph. Pretty, in a sense – her skin as white as parchment, her eyes a dark black-blue – her elfin body looked as if it could contort in any way. Her choice of ill-fitting clothes accentuated her awkward movements. She looked as if, at the slightest confrontation, she would run away out of wilfulness.

'I'm Muriel. You must be Daddy's new private secretary. They don't last long here,' the girl said peremptorily.

'I'm sorry to hear that,' Iris replied.

'But you mustn't be afraid to ask for anything you want,' Muriel continued in her bird-like voice. 'There will always be someone to help you.' But she said this in such a carefree way that Iris felt she meant the opposite.

Iris was due to meet Lady Melfort after breakfast. She

knocked on the door of the drawing room at ten o'clock promptly. As she entered, Lady Melfort was already waiting for her, sitting on a sofa in the centre of a daffodil-coloured room, wearing a shot-silk dress of aquamarine that reminded Iris of the lustrous feathers of the peacock. Although about sixty years old, there was an energy to Lady Melfort's angular features that caught the beauty of her youth. She gaily motioned Iris to sit down beside her. As she did so, Iris noticed her own plain dress was slightly frayed at the hem.

'We don't stand on ceremony here, Iris. Would you mind pouring?' Iris leant over the small table bearing the teapot, picked it up and poured pale tea into two cups, delicately sprigged in forget-me-nots.

'Your secretarial qualifications and references are very impressive, Miss Drummond. When we received them by post, we made the decision to hire you on the spot. And now that I see you in the flesh' – Lady Melfort looked Iris up and down, proprietarily – 'I see that we were absolutely right.'

Iris had grown used to the condescension of her employers. Her ability to detach, she thought, was her one source of strength.

'You look much younger than thirty-five years old,' Lady Melfort continued. 'That's what it said on your *curriculum vitae,* wasn't it? Thirty-five years old. And unmarried.'

'Yes, your Ladyship. '

At her age, Iris thought, she was supposed to have been married by now; she was supposed to have had children. Sometimes she felt like King Midas. Everything she touched turned to gold. Her inability to love transformed everything it touched into metal. But it meant, she thought, that she remained undistracted from what she needed to do. And that she was often surrounded by beautiful, brazen things.

'We thought, because of your age, that you would have sufficient maturity to do the job well. The last one was a bit younger. Emotionally unstable. Apparently it ran in her family. And it *is* difficult to find good people to come out this far into the wilds. Do have a biscuit.'

Daphne's capriciousness, Iris thought, had been part of her allure. Her younger sister had fallen in love easily, passionately, and fallen out of love again with the same lightness. Love had seemed to Daphne arbitrary; something that swept over her and was gone, or drunk like the nectar of the gods, a temporary madness.

Iris took a piece of crumbly shortbread from the proffered plate.

'Of course, you will find Glen Almain a place where people keep to themselves. And as you will be working for the Under-Secretary for War, it would be advisable for *you* to keep to yourself, too.'

Margaret Melfort gave a very direct and charming smile and, as the older woman leant forward, Iris caught the delicate scent of lily of the valley.

Iris glanced around the room. A painting hanging above the mantelpiece attracted her attention. An oil painting of Lady Melfort's family, it depicted Lord and Lady Melfort and, presumably, their two sons, standing amongst classical ruins in a desert landscape. All their expressions seemed lifeless, their figures painted in muted tones.

Lady Melfort noticed Iris looking at the painting.

'My son Edward is the artist. Do you like it, Miss Drummond?'

'It's interesting,' Iris said doubtfully, for the painting seemed too surreal for her logical mind. 'Did he paint it recently?'

'Last year.'

'I wondered, because Muriel isn't in it.'

'He found Muriel difficult to pin down. Everyone does.'

'Why are there broken pillars?' Iris asked.

'Edward tells me they symbolize loyalty.'

'I see.'

'We are a very loyal family, you know, Miss Drummond. It's important in these uncertain times for blood to be thicker than water.' Suddenly Margaret Melfort asked abruptly, 'How did you hear of the job?'

8

'I saw it advertised in *The Times*.'

A parlour-maid entered and began to clear away the plates.

'My husband has left clear instructions for you in the library,' Lady Melfort said. Then she added distractedly, 'Please don't let Xavier give you anything extracurricular.'

'I'll try not to,' Iris replied, puzzled.

Lady Melfort stood up and Iris realized she had been dismissed.

'Just before you go,' Lady Melfort continued, 'I'm afraid there was some kind of misunderstanding over breakfast. The people who work for my husband tend to eat in the kitchen with the other servants. Or you can eat alone in your room, if you prefer.'

Iris left the bright drawing room to find herself in one of the dark corridors of the castle, and bumped into a figure who had been standing just behind the door. She looked up to see a man in his mid-thirties smiling down at her. He was thin and tall – he looked as if his face had been sculpted away. There was something old-fashioned and poetic about him, and that undefinable quality, charm, hung about him like musk. He moved in a feline way, yet without appearing to be in any way sensual. His pale brown hair was swept back from his face and his eyes seemed large and luminous in the dark.

'Hallo. I don't think we have been introduced. I'm Louis.' He had the same languorous phrasing as his mother, but she noticed that his long white fingers were twitching nervously.

'I'm Miss Drummond, your father's new secretary.'

'Ah yes. There have been rumours about you.'

'Good ones, I hope.'

'I couldn't say… Anyway, I don't think there's going to be much for you to do. My father is hardly ever here.' He didn't meet her eyes. There was something about Louis that gave Iris the odd feeling that he wasn't quite there, as if his

9

old character had left him and this thin cut-out was all that remained. Nor, since she had entered the castle, had the unreality of her situation quite left her.

'If you'll excuse me, could you tell me the way to the library?'

Louis simply pointed down the hallway to the door at the end.

The library was a pleasant room lined with mahogany panelling, and overlooked the avenue to the lodge rather than the courtyard and the gardens. There were two desks facing each other, the larger one clearly belonging to Lord Melfort, the other – on which her instructions for the next week or so lay – for his private secretary. She spent the day typing letters and filing various documents. It was only when she worked, Iris thought, that she felt at one with the world around her.

Chapter 3

Over the following weeks, Iris gradually relaxed into the daily routine of the castle. It was a kind of Eden here: Eden before the fall; a paradise, with its extensive gardens and its enclosed formality within the wildness of the surrounding countryside. The castle seemed to offer culture and civilization whereas what had happened to Daphne, Iris thought, must have had a wild and primitive source. There *had* been a fall here: a terrible fall.

Iris chose to eat alone in her room, rather than with the other servants. The food at the castle was always of the highest quality. There was no need for rationing, as the estate was largely self-sufficient. The family lived on the deer, pheasant and hare they shot, as well as the fresh salmon and trout they caught from the river. The choicest fresh vegetables were plucked from the ground, the sweetest fruit picked from the vines or orchards. Freshly-baked bread came straight out of the kitchen's ovens. Even chocolate and coffee were smuggled in, in plentiful supply. The servants either shared in the bounty, or enjoyed the various remains.

During a rainstorm that drenched the skies, Lord Melfort returned to Glen Almain. Iris was summoned to the library where she found an elderly man, lost in thought at his desk. He was like the large oak tree outside his window, she decided: sturdy and definite. Its branches and leaves were clearly-defined, reaching outwards and upwards, a powerful emblem of duty and responsibility.

Having introduced himself, he spoke slowly and carefully while she took the dictation of some rather dull ministerial letters. He then instructed her on how to fend off the press and protect him from people he did not want to deal with.

That afternoon, after being dismissed for the day, Iris looked out of the window to see that the sky had lightened and the rain had stopped. She hurriedly put on her raincoat and stepped outside into the fresh air with a sense of relief. She walked along the avenue until she reached the road that ran along the top of the glen. A rough grassy path led off it, down to the river which threaded through the bottom of the glen. As she skirted a steep cliff on her left, a distant roar like the sound of anger began to fill her head. It was the sound of a waterfall which, as she approached, seemed to replace all of her thoughts with its noise.

She entered a glade and gazed up at the waterfall. The sound flooded out of the glade with a thunderous rushing. Swollen with the deluge of rain, the waterfall tumbled down with ferocity into a large pool below, seeming to crush everything beneath its force. Amidst a morass of swirling foam, the pool was churned up into a fury of water.

Iris began to feel faint. Her flesh seemed to pull away from her bones in the face of such energy. Like the rocks, she felt herself becoming eroded, but replaced by an odd vertiginous strength of her own, stolen from the water. This is what made her feel faint: not fear of the waterfall's power, but the feeling of power itself. As if, all her life, she had hidden from power – and here it was, surging through her. She felt as if the glen were suffusing her with a natural force. And the world started to circle her and the white water turned to black and Iris lost consciousness.

She opened her eyes to find herself lying on the ground, feeling something licking her face. It was the rough tongue of a black and white sheepdog. Iris looked straight into its alert and determined eyes. A few moments later a boy's head, with a shock of white hair, bent down into her line of vision. It was the boy she had seen in the schoolhouse. His face registered no emotion. It was as if he were looking down, not at Iris, but at some sleeping animal that he had expected to find there.

She slowly, unsteadily, rose to her feet. She could feel the warm sun on her face, and the noise of the waterfall had lessened. The dog began to run around her legs, barking. She brushed back her hair and flicked the leaves and fronds of fern from her dress.

'I'm perfectly fine,' she said, although the boy had not asked after her and did not seem curious as to what she had been doing lying on the ground. Something about his watchful rose pink eyes, however, made her want to explain herself.

'My name is Iris. I work for Lord Melfort.'

He was now looking at her intently, as if pursuing her for a meaning that he did not have himself. She began to speak more slowly, but this seemed to annoy him.

'I was watching the waterfall. I must have fainted... It's not like me at all.'

'That's the glen for you,' the boy said, shortly. But he was no longer looking at her; he seemed to be staring just over her left shoulder. The dog began whimpering and he signalled quickly to her.

'Cassie. Heel. She doesn't like it here,' he explained. In spite of his unusual albino colouring, the boy seemed vulnerable, with his grazed knuckles and his dirty nails. He looked uncared-for and unkempt. Iris wanted to comfort him, but her natural reticence held her back. Suddenly, a look of fear crossed his face. 'Cassie can scent a ghost here...'

The boy now seems to be living in a fantasy, Iris thought: a continuous dream of shifting images and plots according to his own making, that no-one else can see or understand.

'It's too late, you know,' he added.

'I'm sorry?'

'She's already gone.'

She shivered. 'Are you talking about Daphne?'

Without replying, he turned away. He trudged back up the path towards the road, his dog following closely at his heels. Grief lay in the way the boy moved: in the slant of his small shoulders, in the slowness of his movements, as if

13

sadness pervaded the air around him and had thickened it as he walked.

Almain Castle had been in Lady Melfort's family since the fifteenth century. Lady Melfort was conscious of her line, of the power of inheritance, but also took great pride in her property and lands. Everything on the estate was about blood – blood spilt and blood related.

She took her guardianship of her workers seriously, expecting absolute loyalty in return for her protection. But Iris had learnt from the lower servants that if one of her workers displeased her she would discharge him without warning, even if his father's father had worked on the estate and his family had lived in the tied house for decades.

One day, Iris was taking a walk in the garden when she looked up and saw Lady Melfort strolling towards her. Peacocks were strutting down the path before her, the imitation eyes of their opened feathers watching Iris carefully.

Iris wondered if Lady Melfort suspected her motives for coming to the castle.

'I would like to show you something,' Lady Melfort said. 'Would you be so good as to come with me?'

Lady Melfort took Iris up the narrow attic steps to the roof of the castle which overlooked the countryside all around, lined by glinting streams. The birds in the sky, against the dark grey clouds, caught a ray of sun and their wings turned to metal.

Iris looked at Lady Melfort's indomitable silhouette as she surveyed her domain.

'Why are there so many ruined houses in the glen, Lady Melfort?'

Without taking her eye off her land, she replied under her breath, 'The estate was given to my family as reward for fighting against the Jacobite cause. My ancestors were then responsible for clearing the glen. Hundreds used to live here. Now there are just sheep and stones and ferns. One day our family will be punished for the clearing of Glen Almain.' Lady Melfort gave a sardonic laugh. 'You see that forest down there?'

Iris looked down across the river at the bottom of the glen and saw a large wood of what looked like pale trees.

'Those are stone trees. Petrified. Some kind of strange animal is supposed to live there.' She looked at Iris for a moment. 'But you, Miss Drummond. You seem to be a very rational person. Always in control of your emotions. I expect you don't believe in that kind of thing.'

'You are correct, Lady Melfort. I believe in rational thought. Only with reason can mankind progress. As long as we have reason, we have nothing to fear. Reason will always master emotion.'

That afternoon Iris descended the flight of steps to the sundial and took the path through the classical archway that led to the kitchen garden. Fruit trees – apples, pears and plums – grew against the upper walls. No-one replied to her knock on the greenhouse's wooden door, and she opened it – to be engulfed in the sweet smell of passion-flowers, peaches and apricots.

Still seeing no sign of anyone, Iris shouted out, 'Is anyone there?' She heard footsteps coming toward her between the trestles of the plants and seedbeds: the soft thuds of heavy boots. As the sun was shining directly in her eyes through the greenhouse glass, she could not at first make out the man's face. Then, as his head blocked out the sun, she saw a face that looked as if it had been encased in stone. He looked invulnerable. He looked as if he were one of the statues in the garden, come to life. The servants had rarely talked to her about the head-gardener, but when they did, they had always talked about him in awed whispers.

'What can I do for you, Miss Drummond?' Hector asked.

'I was just looking around. I hope you don't mind?'

'Why should I?' He started to rearrange the pots on the

15

trestles.

'You've been in Glen Almain long?'

Without looking up, he said, 'All my life. My father and grandfather were head-gardeners, too. I was brought up here. As a child I used to play with Edward, Louis and Muriel – we got up to all sorts of tricks.'

'But you don't associate with them any more?'

He looked up. '*Associate?* What kind of word is that? But no, I don't *associate* with them any more. They come to visit me occasionally. '

Iris looked hesitant. He gave a broad smile. 'You've another question for me?'

'I was wondering about the name of the boy with the white hair and the sheepdog.'

'The albino? That would be Coll. He's not very quick. He doesn't understand things easily.'

That was not the impression Iris had of the boy.

'Who are his parents?'

'He lives with his father, the gamekeeper in the glen. The boy's mother died when he was young. Muriel sometimes plays with him.'

Hector's pale face was surrounded by a mass of golden curls. His eyes were set slightly close together, but he had a long strong nose and full mouth. She swept some earth from her dress; it had brushed against the flowerpots that held the intensely-coloured buttercup yellows and midnight blues of the orchids. The pupils of Hector's eyes in the light were tiny, but the irises were a large expanse of green.

She quickly looked away from his gaze, towards the wild fields beyond the garden. The fields were dissected by the small wooden windows of the greenhouse, and she felt as if she were looking at a puzzle made up of small squares.

16

Chapter 4

A deep-rooted sensitivity allowed Lord Melfort to reach under the skin of women. However, his manners were as smooth as Venetian glass. Women saw him as both understanding and powerful, and this was a combination he used to his advantage. Iris observed with amusement the power he had over the female guests and servants.

Lady Melfort appeared still to be very much in love with her husband, even though her skin was now as lined as the crevices of rock outside the castle gate, and her hair the texture of thin steel wire. She became soft and languorous in his presence. They melded together like earth and water to form a heavy indissoluble clay. Iris quickly realized that at the centre of the castle's life was their unspoken mutual understanding. As heads of estate, they also played a symbolic role. Without their union, the hierarchy of the feudal estate would collapse.

The castle had its own world of aristocratic visitors who came and went in their Bentleys, while Iris and the other servants remained inconspicuous. One morning, soon after the latest visitors had left, Iris was passing the breakfast room when she heard Lady Melfort say, 'So you are going down to London again this week?' The door was ajar and Iris peered through the narrow opening. Her husband looked up from his kippers. Iris could see that he was enjoying the way the flesh flakes were parting between his tongue and the roof of his mouth.

'There's a debate going on at the House of Lords tomorrow. I must be there.'

'You're looking tired, Xavier.'

17

'It's difficult at the moment – that warmonger, Churchill.'

'I don't want another war.' She sighed. 'There's been eighteen years of peace.'

'Germany's rearmament is just about national pride. Nothing more.

'You're too impressionable, Xavier.'

'I'm not alone in thinking this, Margaret. Many in Parliament agree with me. Heinrich is sure we will win the argument for appeasement. '

'Do you believe everything that man says, Xavier?'

She stood up grandly and moved towards the door. Iris walked swiftly on. She could hear Lady Melfort's footsteps clicking imperiously down the corridor behind her, full of confidence and possession, a sense of place; this castle was her history.

Iris decided to explore the long corridors of the castle, and its doors that led off into empty cold rooms filled with dust and fading light. She walked down the worn hall carpet, with its intricate pattern of leaves in pale creams and lilacs. She started to run along the corridor of the East Wing, following its turns right or left as the fancy took her.

She ended up out of breath in front of a heavy oaken door. She looked down the corridor both ways and, seeing no sign of servants or family, she pushed open the door. Behind the door was a room unlike any other that she had ever seen, such was its extravagance and opulence. The room seemed to have been conjured up out of the castle's dreams. The carpet was deep plush green: a damp luxuriant lawn. A crystal chandelier vied with the heavy gilt ornaments around the room for reflecting light. A crimson velvet curtain hung from a huge four poster bed, elaborately painted in lurid colours with scenes from Ovid's *Metamorphoses*. Its wooden posts were carved with thick snake-like vines. The richly ornate room disturbed her, for its very lushness threatened to overwhelm her. And it seemed at odds with the castle's general austerity.

A vase of fresh roses sat on the bedside table. Iris walked over to the table and opened the drawer – a book with a red leather binding lay inside. She picked it up. Its title, embossed in gold read, '*The Art of Falconry.*' Iris opened the book and saw, written on the blank bookplate, bordered by dark green ivy leaves, her sister's name. *Daphne Tennant.* She immediately suppressed any feeling she might have had at seeing her sister's evocative handwriting.

The book was full of coloured illustrations of hawks and falcons, intricate line drawings of the falconer's 'furniture,' and diagrams of various methods of training. Daphne had underlined in red ink the definition of the lure.

'The lure is an imitation, sometimes dead, sometimes live, of a bird attached to a line and used in training before entering a hawk at wild quarry, to teach her some flight techniques and to rehearse her for taking quarry, footing it properly, and resisting the temptation to carry it.'

In the same red ink, Daphne had written in the passage's margin: *Lord Melfort?*

An ebony wardrobe stood at the far wall, the mosaic of its inlaid mirror reflecting back Iris' fragmented face. She walked toward the wardrobe door and opened it. Hanging inside were glamorous dresses of Chinese silks and sequined satins. But slipped in between the shiny luxurious materials were more simple inexpensive dresses, quite out of place. Iris vaguely felt that she recognized them. And then she noticed a woman's plain dark coat and a skirt that she felt certain were Daphne's. She had seen her wearing them frequently. Had this been Daphne's room? It was like a shrine.

She had an overwhelming sense of nausea, and the feeling that something was terribly wrong. Why had her sister's belongings not been returned to her family? Why had the Melforts kept her things? And why, as a mere secretary, had she been living in such luxurious surroundings? It was a bedroom that belonged more to a mistress than a private secretary. The cheap dresses of her dead sister hung down like shrouds.

Iris left the room, quietly shutting the door behind her, and went out into the garden. The roses that lined the paths exuded the same perfume as the roses in Daphne's room. She bent down and inhaled the strong and intense scent. For a moment she lost herself in it. She felt buried alive in its sweetness. The sensation of smell was so powerful that it rose up into her nostrils in an aromatic burst that flooded her mind. She felt as if her thoughts were turning red, the crimson of petals. She looked down at the thorns, sharp, piercing and cruel. Pleasure and pain, the softness, and scent and then the thorns like the claws of a bird of prey.

She suddenly, unfathomably, became frightened of these roses. She stood up and looked around the garden. The roses with their flushing heads seemed eerily static and menacing, their thorns braced outwards, their blooms unseeing. The garden seemed full of their heady scent. The gardener was coming toward her with his slow, swaying gait. Hector was walking down the straight gravel path, between the manicured box hedges.

For a moment, she thought, he doesn't look human. He looks like a god that has been sent down to mingle amongst the mortals. She felt as if she could see straight through him, that he had become transparent, and the garden was the form and substance of him and the vague outline of his figure was the only remaining trace of his masculinity. A pagan god.

His malachite eyes looked almost vacant, as if possessed. He is drunk on his own garden, she thought; intoxicated by the beauty of his creation. He did not see anything sinister in his work of art; no snake in his Garden of Eden.

Chapter 5

Having spent a day typing out official letters, Iris decided to go for a walk in the glen, and took the path that led back down to the waterfall. The leaves whispered all around the small glade. For a moment, Iris thought she saw a hazy figure between the trees, before it disappeared into the shadows. I'm going mad, she thought: it looked like Daphne. The glen's shifting light is playing tricks on my mind.

She heard a mewing sound, like the crying of a baby. She looked up, and saw a buzzard circling with its huge wings outspread against the white of the sky. She would see these birds hunched over dead rabbits in the fields. Ugly dark brown birds, their feathers as lustreless as a dull day. Their sing-song mewing gave voice to the empty space above.

The now-tranquil waterfall was falling into the large pool below. It hadn't rained for days and all trace of the waterfall's power had gone. Smooth cream and brown stones nestled at the bottom of the amber pool like speckled eggs. At the deepest part of the pool, big sharp-edged rocks were mounted in a surround of golden pebbles.

Branches of oak trees hung over the edge of the pool, trailing their leaves in the water. Grass reeds clustered around the water, their blades sharp and resonant. Iris looked into the pool again. For a moment, she saw her sister lying on her back in the pool, her golden hair splayed out around her. She was naked, her eyes wide open, looking through the water into the wide expanse of sky above. Then the image dissolved.

Iris pulled her grey dress up over her head. A pigeon cooed above her reassuringly. She removed all her clothes and

21

approached the side of the pool. She felt almost possessed. She dived into the water, its coldness seizing her breath. She surfaced, gasping, half-laughing with the icy shock to her body. The oak trees above rustled; the wood pigeon flew out with a rush of throbbing wings.

As she glanced up at the bird, she caught sight of a man sitting in the shadows at the far end of the pool on an outcrop of rocks. He must have been sitting there all the time, his dark clothes camouflaging his body in the gloom. She could feel her cheeks burning with shame at her nakedness – not used to the attention of men, her sensuality haunted her.

Treading water, she asked, 'How long have you been sitting there?'

'Do you mean how long have I been watching you?'

She just stared at him.

'Since you arrived at the pool. You seemed lost in your own world. I didn't want to disturb you.'

Edward Melfort was much more vivid than she had expected. He had a strong sensual face with thick lips and fleshy cheeks and high colouring. Unlike the tenuous Louis, Edward appeared to be almost frighteningly present. His heavy jaw and high forehead, overhung with a mass of chestnut hair, were almost animalistic. She wondered why he had depicted himself so neutrally in his painting of his family.

'I would have preferred it if you *had* disturbed me. At least, before I had taken my clothes off.'

Edward smiled. 'You undressed so quickly, before I knew what was happening.'

'Well, would you mind turning your back to me now?'

He swivelled round on the rock. Iris climbed out of the pool and pulled her dress quickly over her head. With his back still turned to her, he said,

'You know, my father's previous secretary, Daphne, used to like doing things like that. Going swimming, naked. But you seem a very different type. Much more buttoned-up. What on earth possessed you?'

22

Now that Edward had his back to her, he could not see her face.

'Was she the one who killed herself?' she asked, dryly. It was the only information her family had received from the Melforts: that Daphne had killed herself. Both she and her father had been out of the country at the time, and the burial had taken place soon after, without them.

'So one of the lower maids has been gossiping? It was last July. One of the maids noticed Daphne had been acting strangely. Then she went missing.'

'Who found her?'

'Coll discovered her remains a week later, in the petrified forest. Can I turn round now? The view of these trees is becoming boring.'

There was a blustery freshness to the air and the material of the dress was clinging damply to her skin.

'I suppose so,' she said.

Edward turned round again and looked at her. Her dress revealed the shape and contours of her body. As she left the glade, she was aware of him watching her walk away.

Chapter 6

The curlews' song was like the sound of a musical note dropping down a well. The various birdsongs of the glen offered another dimension to the world, and in the heat of the summer day, Iris felt as if she were swooning. A cabbage white butterfly fluttered over the field. She lay down in the grass next to the road and looked up into the sky.

A face loomed over her: Hector's face. He was holding in his arms a box of fruit and vegetables.

'I'm just distributing the leftovers to the estate cottages.'

She stood up hurriedly. Green streaks wound up her ivory muslin dress, in spirals. Without saying anything he handed her a raspberry punnet, the wooden sides stained with raspberry juice, which in turn stained her hands when she took them. The sun had brought out the crushed raspberries' sweet smell. She could never look at Hector directly. She felt that, if she looked at him, she would turn to stone and never be able to look away again.

She heard him laugh.

'What is it?' She managed finally to meet his gaze.

He didn't answer. He put his hand to her hair and pulled out a few blades of grass. A hawk lifted itself up to the sky.

'There's the falconer's bird,' he said.

To her surprise, Hector's face had gone very still, as if it had been submerged under cold water.

'The falconer?' she asked.

'He's not from here. We don't know where he came from. He just turned up one day. He's been here for many years. He lives on what his birds fetch him. He does odd jobs around the estate – mends fences, feeds the grouse. His hawks kill the crows that eat the grouse eggs. But he does a bit of poaching on the moor, too, so he avoids the gamekeeper. The falconer's seen as a bit of a loner.'

'Did he know Daphne Tennant well?'

'The falconer taught Daphne falconry.'

Hector looked at her. His green-grey eyes seemed to have more depth than normal. 'In fact, the falconer became infatuated with her. Daphne besotted men. Actually, it was a kind of curse. No man could resist her. She cast spells on everyone she met.'

'Including you?'

'I am different.'

She realized with utmost certainty that she could trust him. He would not tell anyone. Hector belonged to the natural world. He was not interested in human society.

'I've come to the glen to find out why Daphne killed herself. Daphne was my sister.'

Hector stared at her for a moment, and then said, 'It must have been a terrible shock for you, her death.'

A blankness overcame her, as if she just had been buried in snow. But Daphne had been a kind of Icarus, flying close to the sun.

Condensation formed at the window, and the glass clouded over as if the world outside had turned opaque. The first leaves were beginning to fall, and there was an air of panic – as if the onset of autumn was telling time to speed up after the languor of the summer days. Time had become a rush towards the death of living things. The indulgent stupor of summer was over and it was time for activity, even if it should be in the direction of death and coldness. Iris felt as if she were falling under the spell of Glen Almain. She was beginning to feel that only by finding out what had happened to Daphne could she break the spell and leave.

Like a map of the glen – lines, dots, grids on paper – Daphne's death seemed to be more symbolic than real. Tragedies were too painful to admit into the fabric of daily life.

But Iris knew that she had to work out the details of the map; read the symbols carefully. Daphne's suicide had been the result of some kind of breakdown – of that she was sure. Daphne had skated along the surface of life, performing pirouettes and figures of eight. Daphne would have been convinced that the ice would hold, not realizing it had grown fragile as a sheet of glass.

One morning in early September, Lord Melfort looked up from his desk at Iris.

'Hitler's peace speech has made the injustice of the Versailles Treaty obvious,' he announced. 'We cannot continue this idea of "Victor and Vanquished." It's *obvious* that Hitler doesn't want war. All he wants is peace for a regenerated Germany. A raise in the standard of living for his people. And, of course, the majority of the British people concur with me.'

Iris was impressed by his quiet conviction.

She passed most of autumn researching for Lord Melfort in the library. Occasionally, taking a walk in the garden, she felt sure that someone was staring at her. Glancing up at the castle, she would see the figure of an older woman looking down at her, always from the same window in the East Wing. She seemed to be wearing a long white gown, like a prophetess. She had a still, inexpressive face which would disappear as quickly as the moon behind a cloud.

Iris also continued her exploration of the castle. One afternoon, she wandered into a different part of it. She found herself walking down the narrow corridors of the servants' quarters on the ground floor. She entered an ante-room on what appeared to be the far side, and let out a gasp.

Portraits of children hung all around the walls of the small chamber. The children's ivory flesh seemed to glow against the painted black backgrounds. Some lay as babies, swaddled, wrapped in thick cloth. Other, older, children stood stiffly caught in time and the style of the time, their eyes wide open, with an expression of guilelessness. As if they were not seeing the world in front of them, but their own innocence reflected back.

'*These are all portraits of children who died young.*'

She wasn't sure if these words had been spoken out loud or were the thoughts in her head. She turned around, and saw Edward. His pale blue eyes looked at her possessively, as if she had become another object in the castle that he could judge or assimilate. He was handsome, she thought; like a chivalrous medieval knight. But she was not here to be rescued.

'Quite a morbid little hobby of my mother's, don't you think? Collecting pictures of dead children. She only began it last year. Here in the glen, the mothers of illegitimate children used to kill their babies and bury them under the floorboards. Anything, rather than face the shame. They would then say that the fairies had carried their babies away at night, to the other side.'

Something in his voice made Iris look at him hard. Edward walked back toward the door on the other side of the room.

'You seem lost.'

Iris did not like to admit to any weakness.

'What do you mean?' she asked, defensively.

'Literally lost, as if you don't know where you are.'

She laughed. 'Of course I do. We're at the far end of the castle.'

He pointed to the doors of the chamber, one in each wall.

'Which is the room that leads back, then?'

She went over to the door on the west side and opened it. The flames of the fire that flickered in from the drawing room caused shadows to play over the faces of the children, as if they were ablaze. She must have walked round the castle's corridors in a circle.

Edward smiled.

'If I were you, I would go in to the drawing room. You look cold. '

One chilly morning when she was working alone in the library, Edward came in to interrupt her reverie.

'Would you like to go sailing, Iris? We have a small boat moored on the loch.'

The loch was as still as a looking-glass. As Edward prepared the boat, a slight breeze stirred the water and her hair. She observed his strong hands and easy practiced movements. Unlike Louis, he was certain of his physical strength, confident of what he could do with his body. He was lucky, she thought, not to have been wounded in the war. His physical persona determined his character; his flesh and bone defined who he was. The sail, flapping like a large swan's wing, was hoisted with just a few strong pulls of his arm.

Iris sat to the prow and Edward sailed the boat out into the loch. The mountains that surrounded the loch were grand and stark. The landscape had transmuted into the silvers and golds of November. Vegetation was sparse, and the pale stone trees of the petrified forest in the distance stood out against the dark earth. It was a cold, almost icy day, the sun a white bright coin in the sky. There was very little wind; no animals, no sound of birds. Just the boat running through the loch, the water lapping musically against the clinker-built stern.

The wind began to blow more strongly against her cheeks and the boat picked up speed. For the first time since she had arrived in the glen she felt truly carefree. She felt as if she were a bird soaring in the air, then flying low, skimming close to the water.

Edward saw the look of joy on her face and gave her a broad grin.

'I better warn you, I'm a hedonist.'

'And does pleasure come to you often?' Iris asked, dryly.

'Ah,' Edward teased, 'I hear disapproval in your tone. Do you not approve of pleasure?'

She did not reply. She had always been disconnected from herself – even more so since her sister's death. He gave her another smile. His clothes hung loosely on him, as if he were trying to shed them, as if his clothes were various skins or shells from which he was longing to emerge. She repressed a strong urge to lean her head backward slightly, away from Edward, over the water.

'You're quite the Puritan, aren't you, Miss Drummond? Unlike your predecessor.'

Iris had to remind herself that he did not know who she was. She seized her chance. 'If Miss Tennant enjoyed her life so much, why did she end it?'

Edward shrugged his shoulders. 'Her suicide note didn't explain.'

'A suicide note? What exactly did it say?' she asked. *Her death in writing.*

'I can't remember. It was a few inconsequential words. The police discovered it in the drawer of her bedside table and an hour later they'd lost it.'

'Her note went *missing*?' She heard laughter, and looked across the loch to see Coll and Muriel playing on the isle.

'It had been left on the hall table. I saw Louis hovering round… Louis is like a magpie – he likes to steal. Things often go missing in the castle. He collects stuff for his Cabinet of Curiosities: jewellery, other bits and bobs.'

'Didn't the police think it a bit odd that her note had vanished?'

'How do you think we kept the police out of it as much as we did? Have you any idea what power mother's wealth gives her?' He gave a sardonic laugh. 'My mother didn't want any fuss surrounding Daphne Tennant's suicide. A suicide in the glen was highly embarrassing for her. She's fiercely controlling and protective of the Almain Estate. She was furious that there had been a death at all, and she wanted it all over with quickly. There was no inquest. The coroner returned a verdict of suicide within a week and the funeral happened a few days later. And that was that. Mother is fiercely protective of her privacy and her good name.'

'It was as if she took it personally?'

'Yes. It was as if she took it personally.'

He paused, then said, 'You're quite an inquisitive person, Iris. For a secretary. Aren't secretaries just supposed to take dictation?'

She smiled. 'Oh, we can think for ourselves too.'

He looked into her eyes with his own – his blue, always slightly distant eyes – and she wondered if he were beginning to suspect who she was. Edward had obviously known Daphne quite well; there must have been tiny elements of Daphne that he saw in her. The two sisters had been different in many ways, but did they perhaps have a similar scent, or incline their head in the same way? But Edward, she thought, did not notice the details of women.

The sound of Coll and Muriel playing on the isle once again carried over to the boat.

'Voices carry easily over water. People forget that,' Edward said, quietly.

Iris looked out of the window that night and saw Muriel dancing like a fairy in the garden.

Chapter 7

The following morning, Iris decided to continue further down the glen road. Having ambled for about a mile, she noticed a chapel, covered in winter roses, on top of a small hill. A few sheep that were grazing there had escaped from the neighbouring field. Coll was trying to round them up, whistling to Cassie in piercing swoops of sound. Cassie had cornered a particularly uncooperative sheep, and was neatly bringing it into a stone-walled pen. Cassie was alive as the wind seemed alive; a quick spirit moved through her. Then she patiently waited by the pen gate. When still, she looked as if all her restrained force was about to be unleashed.

In the shadow of the ancient pines, the chapel looked picturesque. The Victorian building was simply built, with a single stained glass window, framed by shutters. A young woman was crossing over the hill, heading toward the entrance of the chapel. The dark coat and gloves she was wearing looked incongruous in the countryside, but the woman's fair hair was loose, falling down around her shoulders. Her feet were bare. The woman was wearing the same town clothes Daphne had used to wear: the same dark coat and skirt that Iris had seen hanging in the wardrobe at Almain castle. Iris became convinced that it was Daphne. A sense of fervid hope overcame her.

Daphne was leading her to the chapel, and Iris started to run up the small hill after her. Daphne opened the big door and disappeared inside. Iris, a hundred yards behind, reached the top of the hill and followed her in. Breathless, she looked around the chapel for her younger sister.

Morning light illuminated the interior. Dust motes swam

in the wintry light. A dark brown leather bible had been left on each oaken pew. A pile of bibles was also stacked up on one of the windowsills. But there was no sign of Daphne, and Iris fought off a feeling of desolation.

She went over to the visitors' book that lay open on a plinth in a corner of the chapel. The most recent signature was *Heinrich Berger* – presumably the same man that the Melforts had been talking about at breakfast.

She idly flicked through the pages, noting the dates. There were not many names, as Glen Almain did not attract many visitors. She stopped on July 16th 1935, a few days before her sister had died. And there it was: her sister's signature, beneath another signature of Heinrich Berger's. Daphne had written something beside her signature, and with difficulty – for Daphne's handwriting seemed distressed – Iris deciphered the word, *Gruinard*.

Just then, Iris heard the click of the latch to the chapel's main door, and she turned, and saw Lady Melfort enter. Lady Melfort hovered at the entrance a moment before spotting Iris. She looked surprised and aggrieved to see her there, as if she, rather than Iris, had been interrupted. She began walking down the aisle towards her, her grey hair – struck by the light through the windows – a silver halo.

'So what are you doing here?' Lady Melfort never worried about sounding peremptory. She thought that answers to her direct questions were her birthright.

Iris replied, 'I saw the chapel from the road. I was curious.'

Sunlight was now streaming through the stained glass window, lighting up the Mediterranean blues, grass-greens and ochre-yellows in a blazing mosaic of intensely-coloured glass. Light was illuminating the three biblical scenes: Abraham about to sacrifice Isaac, the angel coming down to prevent Abraham cutting Isaac's throat, and Abraham offering up the ram as sacrifice instead.

'During the Great War, everyone in the glen lost cousins, uncles, fathers and sons,' Lady Melfort said. 'We know about sacrifice here. The Scots lost the highest proportion of men in any country in the war. We lost Louis.'

'I don't understand.'

'I don't mean *lost* in the conventional way. Louis wasn't *killed*. But the old Louis has gone forever. Shell-shock did terrible things to his mind. The mustard gas has destroyed any chance of him having children. Xavier can't accept how Louis has changed. Never will. Louis is the eldest son, you know.'

'I thought it was Edward,' Iris exclaimed.

'Edward came back a war hero. He will inherit. Louis could never run an estate now.'

'Is that why I never see the brothers together?'

Lady Melfort looked at her.

'Not entirely. It is more to do with my husband's previous secretary. She came between them. Since then, they hardly speak. I think, in some way, each blames the other for her death.'

Lady Melfort looked at her slyly. 'Actually, you look a bit like her.' Her eyes were as hard as the stony pebbles at the bottom of the pool.

'Would you excuse me, Lady Melfort?' Iris said.

Leaving Lady Melfort inside, she left the chapel. A small graveyard lay at the back of the chapel: a few ancient tombstones dotted about amongst the pines. She noticed that one of the headstones was smoother and more recently embedded than the others. Iris slowly approached it. The inscription simply read:

DAPHNE TENNANT 1906 – 1935.
REST IN PEACE.

Iris refused to feel pain. She refused to feel anything. She had never felt love for her sister. Her eyes felt dry. Full of the opposite of tears. Grief had not occurred to her. It was not what she would allow herself. Grieving was the letting of

33

everything else fall away. Grief was the shedding of hope.

But what precisely had happened to her sister in the glen? Who had she associated with? Who had she loved? What had she found out? Iris was no nearer to understanding the quotidian details of her life. But she would try, by osmosis, to feel her sister's presence, understand her in a way that she had never tried to do while Daphne was alive.

She would build a castle of her sister's last few days. It would be made of stone, as real as the castle that lay at the end of the avenue lined with the vertebrae of silver-boned beeches.

One day in early December, Iris was taking dictation from Lord Melfort in his library. It was a place of refuge for her, with the bookcases lining the walls and the wood fire crackling. Lord Melfort sat behind his desk, kindly and distant, treating her with extreme courtesy and revealing none of his private thoughts.

'I can see you are slightly bored with your secretarial duties, Miss Drummond.'

'It's just the time of year, Lord Melfort. It makes me slightly restless.'

'I'm sure, with a girl of your intellect, that it's a bit more than that. Might you not be interested in something more challenging? Perhaps undertake for me some further research? I noted on your *curriculum vitae* that you speak very good German. You could ask the German ministry to send us press releases of Goebels' speeches. You could also check for statements that express peaceful intentions from the German Ministers of War and Ministers of Science and Technology. I want to use them in speeches in the House to acknowledge German's good will and sincerity.'

'Anything to help the cause of appeasement, Lord Melfort.' Iris had seen the wounded soldiers being wheeled down the streets of London; the grieving mothers and children.

'Asking you to do this is obviously an acknowledgement of the high esteem I hold you in, Iris. You see, I don't want this done through the department. I want you to deal with this personally. Otherwise I would have to discuss it with the Foreign Office and the press departments of our embassies. Your helping me in this way will save a lot of trouble and inconvenience.'

Just before they were about to stop for the day, Iris looked up from assembling her notes and asked, 'Lord Melfort, what does *Gruinard* mean?'

He hesitated. 'It's an island off the west coast of Scotland.'

'Is there anything special about it?'

'It's a research station.'

'For what?'

He stood up and put some papers in his briefcase.

'It's a testing ground for biological weapons. Experiments on sheep, that sort of thing.'

As Iris lay in bed that night, the glen beyond the garden reminded her of death. It was a wild place with no laws, no time for sentimentality. At night the owls, with a moth-like beating of their wings, hunted their prey.

She fell asleep and dreamed of a hawk coming down over her sister's face, of it mantling, spreading its wings over her face as its talons penetrated her scalp, so that Iris could not see how it was feeding on her sister's face.

Chapter 8

While the Melfort family was abroad for Christmas and the New Year, Iris spent a freezing December and January secluded in the library, in front of a roaring fire. She enjoyed the peace and solitude, and proceeded to lose herself in her work. She began annotating the Führer's speeches, for Lord Melfort's future use in the House. Hitler's speeches stated clearly that paramilitary forces such as the *Schutzstaffel* were simply political organizations. Germany's air force expansion was only for civilian use. The more research that she did for Lord Melfort, the more she became convinced that Germany was only interested in peace.

February turned the countryside pale brown and pink. As she walked through the glen one early morning, the combination of potent scents and the imagery of life made her feel light-headed. The flowers had not yet come out, but the trees were turning purple, with dilating buds. The streams caught the sunlight in silver flashes. The whole glen seemed to have melted, to have become less still and icy. There was a movement, and a sense of growing that had not been seen in the glen since winter began. It was as if the earth was becoming less hard, the soil stirring beneath the stunted grass.

It was then that she saw the hawk flying low over the trees – fast. Crashing into an oak, the bird's wings became entangled in the branches. Both bird and tree became locked in a violent struggle. The tree seemed to have a life of its own, fighting to keep the hawk trapped within its lattice of leaves.

The more the hawk struggled, the more the tree fought.

When the hawk would fall still from exhaustion, cruelly the tree would stop fighting too, as if taunting it. Iris watched, half-captivated, at the impossibility of the hawk's situation.

A few moments later she heard the sound of hurried footsteps, and a man came running out of the wood. He stopped to brush the hair back from his sweating forehead. He had a deeply-structured face, as if made of shadows rather than skin. His long dark hair was lanky and hung about his shoulders. He was scrawnily built and his shirt was unbuttoned at the top to reveal a hairless body, pale brown skin like the hide of a young animal. He was like a satyr, Iris thought.

Looking up at the hawk, he said quietly, 'She's a young bird, not fully trained.'

He quickly ascertained, by the movement of its wings, that the bird had not been injured. He walked over to the tree and seemed to embrace the trunk for a moment before quickly climbing up three or four branches to where the hawk was trapped. He carefully parted the tree, and the hawk flew out and landed on the ground, its feathers ruffled. The falconer jumped quietly down to the earth, stretched out his arm, and the hawk fluttered onto it. There was something so graceful in the way the falconer moved and anticipated the bird's movements. The hawk looked almost eerily calm now, as if its state of shock had been replaced by somnambulance.

'So you work for Lord Melfort?' the falconer asked Iris.

'As a secretary and research assistant.'

'It's military development, isn't it? Lord Melfort could learn from the peregrine falcon, a perfect airborne killing machine. She can stoop at two hundred miles an hour.' Iris was surprised by his knowledge of Lord Melfort's work.

'It's not that kind of military development,' she said.

'Does he work you hard?'

'At times, but I have time to myself, too.'

'Well, you'll find nothing to do here but rural pursuits.' The falconer gave a strange laugh.

He tied his young hawk by a creance to a tree stump,

and then whistled. A peregrine falcon flew out of the wood towards him and soared up into the white sky, scanning the earth for movement. The falconer seemed to split in two; his legs and feet were rooted to the ground but the top half of his body was poised as if about to take off in flight. Seeing its prey, the falcon dropped down, let go of its resistance to gravity as the earth pulled it down towards itself.

The bird of prey brought out its talons as it fell. The claws came out, ever retractable, piercing, and plunged into the rabbit's back, through the fur, down into the flesh, the bird's claws like weapons, feeling the pressure of the animal as it resisted and squirmed on its talons, the warm blood trickling over its feet. Then up, the weight of the animal heavy, the falcon's wings beating faster and stronger as it pulled itself and its prey upwards again into the air. The rabbit was still conscious as the falcon brought it down to ground nearby and began stabbing at its throat, its eyes, pulling strips of flesh from the bone.

The falconer walked over to the feasting bird and swiftly pulled the rabbit out of its claws. He tucked the fat buck into his belt, took out a dead chick from his satchel and gave it to the bird as reward for its kill. Iris noticed a slight crooked-ness about the falconer's back: a suggestion of hunchback, of wings folded.

He turned to Iris again with a fierce look.

'So this amuses you?'

'As long as I'm just watching.'

'Are you sure that's what you're doing?'

'What do you mean?'

'Just watching. You might get involved without realizing it.'

Iris watched the falcon pulling on the yellow chick, observed its piercing yellow eyes like balls of gold, the hungry, specific movements of its claws and beak, and the darting movement of its neck and head.

Iris decided that she had to read Daphne's suicide note for

herself. She wanted to read her exact words. If Louis had hidden it in his Cabinet of Curiosities, she needed to see it. One evening, after dinner, she encountered Louis in the corridor.

'Edward tells me that you have a Cabinet of Curiosities.'

A light came into Louis' fugitive dark eyes, like candlelight flickering over deep water. They intrigued and disconcerted Iris at the same time.

'Would you like to see my collection, Miss Drummond?'

'I would, very much. Thank you.'

Louis eagerly took her up to his room on the third floor. He opened the door and, curious, she entered. Candlelight flickered round the room, throwing shadows over the high walls. The whole room had been turned into a Cabinet of Curiosities.

Hanging from the ceiling was a plethora of stuffed animals: a slim, grey hammerhead shark swam through the air. A mobile of brightly-coloured exotic birds dangled down from the chandelier. The ceiling was covered in a *trompe l'oeil* of the night sky, while the floor was chequered like a chessboard in black and white stone tiles.

But it was the huge Cabinets against each wall that dominated the room. The entire room, apart from an area for a bed, armchair and wardrobe, had been turned into a museum. Each cabinet had drawers and also open shelves, laden with objects set out like artefacts in an art exhibition.

One shelf, marked *naturia*, glistened with precious and semi-precious stones in rose-pinks, purples and lapis lazuli. Hybrid beasts bristled on another shelf, sporting assorted spines and scales: an animal with a beak and feathered wings trailed a lizard's tail. She turned to Louis for some explanation. His face was full of wonder, suffused with pleasure, as if his eyes were feasting on a visual banquet.

'The rare and the beautiful are here,' he said proudly.

He opened a cupboard labelled *Artificia*, tenderly took down a small piece of burnt orange coral from a shelf, and placed it on her hand. 'Coral is the skeleton of an animal metamorphosed into a plant. It's supposed to ward off the evil eye.' Minute birds had been carved out of the coral's tentacles, their wings outstretched in flight.

Picking up an amber paperweight, Iris noticed an animal hair trapped inside the amber. Louis handed her a magnifying glass. *'May all your dreams come true'* was engraved on the hair.

'You must have been collecting for years!'

'Since the end of the War. I can no longer work, so I do this instead. An agent helps by travelling the world for me, looking for precious objects.'

Louis pointed to a small black onyx box inlaid with mother-of-pearl and shell. 'He found this in the Seychelles. It holds sacrificed human hearts.' A creamy wax model of a hand, which looked uncannily life-like, held a stuffed wren. 'This,' Louis said, 'represents the Platonic image of memory.'

In spite of the careful labels describing each object, nature and artifice seemed confused in this room, Iris thought. How to order hybrid creatures, fingers of saints, and poison antidotes poison taken from the stomachs of Persian goats? It was a deeply irrational place, made to look rational with its particular categorization and labelling.

'It's all authentic. Unlike some other collections I could tell you about. I know of one collector who ripped the claws off his stuffed bird of paradise!'

'Why?'

'Because, as well as being the symbol of sexual love, the bird of paradise is supposed to be a mythical bird of *flight*. Claws are only for birds that walk.' Louis laughed.

On top of the most ornate cabinet in the room, Iris noticed an elaborate castle of coral, shell and crystal, in the shape of Almain castle. She went over to the cabinet and tried one of the lower drawers. Inside were rows of further smaller drawers, and she pulled one out. Tiny inanimate objects lay on black crushed velvet, all meticulously labelled in Louis's delicate handwriting: whorled shells, the skulls of stoats, feathers, bat wings, fools gold, miniature eggs and the exquisitely-tailored clothes of the fairy-folk made out of snakeskin. A yellowing animal's tooth was labelled: *Found in the petrified forest. Belonged to the beast of Glen Almain.*

The cabinet was Louis' recreation of the natural world of the glen. The war has made him lose his mind, Iris thought.

Iris pulled at another one of the smaller drawers, but it was firmly locked. 'Why is this one locked?' she asked.

'Do you really not understand what kind of place you have come to?'

There was a close, dusty feel to the room, and she was beginning to find it difficult to breathe. A feeling of claustrophobia was overwhelming her, surrounded as she was by these relics of nature. She felt she was becoming petrified, like one of the objects herself, as if her life force was gradually draining out of her. However, surrounded by his wondrous objects, Louis was growing ever more invigorated, as if meaning was slowly being restored to him. His gestures were becoming increasingly pronounced.

It was dawning on Iris that she was simply another object of the natural world, and once dead would become another segment of hair or bone. She would belong inside the Cabinet of Curiosities, as one of the many objects Louis could add to his moonstruck, small world.

Chapter 9

The primroses were breaking out of the soil, the yellow petals cocooned in their shell of green leaves. The ancient red bracken was as brittle as broken bones. And then the first showers for weeks fell: cold fresh rain, bathing the earth and the flowers and leaves.

One morning, soon after the rain had stopped, Iris was working in the library when she caught sight of Louis leaving the castle for a walk. She decided to follow him. Keeping her distance, she clambered over ditches and stone walls after him. Louis, Iris thought, seemed to move all over the glen, through the castle, in and out of the forest and the glades. He was like a shadow that flickered over these places, not really at home anywhere, just a shadow of the things or people already present.

When he reached the river at the bottom of the glen, Louis came to a halt on the pebbly shore, and stood gazing into the water. Iris sat down on a large boulder, a few hundred yards down the shore, partially obscured by trees. Time slowly passed and he did not move from his trance-like position. Out of boredom, she started to study the crevices that criss-crossed the rock. Suddenly, as if out of her imagination, she noticed a dark sinuous movement, and something slipped out of one of the cracks and snaked towards her.

Iris screamed. Louis turned around and saw her clinging to the rock, petrified. She could only watch as he ran over, and with one violent kick knocked the snake to the ground. The stunned snake lay, as if dead, at his feet. Louis lifted up his foot and stamped on the snake's delicate skull, his eyes possessed. The snake's brains oozed out onto the stones like grey spawn. For a moment Iris and Louis were silent as they looked down together at the dead snake, black and white hieroglyphics marking its skin.

'It's spring, Iris. You don't want to be bitten by an adder in Spring. Their heads are full of venom. What were you doing? Spying on me?'

'I just followed you down, that's all.'

As they began their slow walk home, she realized that the incident had affected him more than she had first thought. An unnatural calmness was coming over Louis and his face had grown strangely pale. Abruptly he came to a halt. He was in profile to her.

'Louis,' she said quietly.

He still did not move. His arms hung limply by his side.

She thought at first that he was playing a game with her. She grew unnerved. She moved around so she was standing in front of him and could look straight into his eyes. What she saw made her feel cold inside. She saw fear. The kind of fear that makes everything else leave – a vacation of the soul. Everything about him was deadly still, except the fear in his eyes.

The fear froze her – it was contagious – she felt fearful too, as if he had transmitted it to her like a disease. She took a step back, tried to regain a sense of distance and therefore separateness between them. She thought, I have to help him, shake him out of this trance, retrieve who he is.

She took his arm suddenly in both hands. With a vehement move he shook his arm free, and at the same time knocked her to the ground. Her head just missed a grey rock that was protruding from the grass. A few drops of blood softly seeped from her cheek where she had grazed the ground. She rose unsteadily to her feet.

He started to shout out what at first seemed to her to be gibberish, and then a foreign language she didn't know. Then, slowly, she began to make out the names of men: *Donaldson, Macnab, Moncrieff, Fraser* – he was reciting a list of men's names; he was naming the war dead. Louis then fell to the

43

ground and lay thrusting to and fro on his back in a violent seizure. She bent down over his trembling limbs as his arms flailed as if fighting off invisible assailants.

He fell still. He has died, she thought at first – but she could see his chest rise and fall. He had lapsed into a deep sleep. She knelt down on the grass beside him, watching him, his face fallen into a state of absolute repose. She tried to compose her unquiet thoughts.

That afternoon, as Iris passed the drawing room where Louis was recovering on the sofa, she could hear furious talk coming from inside.

She could hear Lady Melfort saying, 'You must stay away from this woman. I don't like her. She doesn't understand our ways.'

'Iris and I are not your concern, mother – it's none of your business.'

'I am your mother. I have your best interests at heart. And we have to talk about Daphne. It dominates your life. It dominates *our* lives.'

'*No,*' Louis shouted.

Iris could hear his mother approaching the door, and swiftly she walked on.

Daphne oppressed this place, she thought: she haunted it.

The War had taught Louis fear and it now motivated him. He had learnt well. And no matter what he did, fear accompanied him, leaping about his body like a mischievous elf. He would try and shrug the elf off, but he knew that although the elf perched on his shoulder, darted between his ankles, tripped him up and tipped his hat over his eyes, its home was inside his chest and his ribs were its bars.

Louis sometimes thought it was so obvious he was fearful, it was disturbing how few people noticed. He was always amazed by what people didn't notice. As if there was a parallel universe in which the things only he noticed, existed.

44

He was the only one who could enter this universe. Back on earth, his fear and anxiety were the animate forms of this parallel dimension.

Fear was always at the pit of his stomach. Could he call it an emotion? It felt more like a statement of being or a religion – his religion of fear. It seemed to be at the base of every emotion he had: joy, pain excitement, lust, boredom. Always, at the root of these sensations, was a hollow feeling at his core, the hollowness that felt almost like anticipation or lack of fulfilment or desire, but was actually a merciless, irreducible panic.

Louis returned to his room on the third floor of the castle. He was safe in his Cabinet of Curiosities. He wondered why he ever left this place. The outside world was too dangerous and unpredictable. He wanted a smaller horizon. He wanted the limits of his walls. When he looked up, he needed to see the painted night-sky above him and the talismans of his security around him. Only Daphne had understood.

The April sunlight shone through the birch trees, casting shadows on the path that bordered the river. Along the edge of the water, grey stones mottled with dark green lichen crouched like toads. A heron stood perched on a stone in the centre of the river. It was as still as a statue, lithe and emblematic. With its long thin neck and slender etiolated body, the bird was like a shadow of itself.

A pheasant flew up from the grass just beneath Iris' feet with a screaming squawk, making her heart miss a beat. She watched it fly low and ungainly over a field towards the river, where it curved away from its path, wings clumsily and noisily flapping. There were a few seconds of silence in the glen, and then she heard a sound of a different kind. It was a howling; an oddly enticing cry, belonging to a dog, perhaps: Coll's dog. The sound was coming from the petrified forest on the other side of the river. An old iron bridge spanned the river a few yards down from where she was. The howling was growing louder. It now felt for an uncanny moment as

45

if it were coming from within her, the ululation sounding a wretched mixture of the human and animal. She followed the howling over the bridge.

Iris stopped at the edge of the large forest of fossilized trees. The outline of the stony trees with their sharp spiky branches pierced the sky, their sepulchral bare beauty alien and unnatural. The pale stone trees were like skeletal monuments to the dead; testament to lost life. The crying stopped.

The statues seem to be quietly observing her as Iris took a walk in the gardens. She looked up at Almain Castle and thought how, with its history of wealth and conflict, it must be full of hidden and distorted passion. When the castle and the wildness of the glen met there was bound to be conflict, a tempest, death.

One of the statues that peeped over a circular hedge caught her eye. The sculpture seemed to have moved off-centre. Entering the hedge, Iris saw that the statue of the woman appeared to have shifted at least five feet to one side. Iris heard footsteps, and turned; Edward was there. She immediately wondered if he had been following her. However, instead of acknowledging her, he just stood staring in front of the statue, as if in a trance.

As Iris gazed more closely, she could see that the statue's legs joined into a single stone tree-trunk whose roots were spreading out into the pedestal beneath her. The lower half of her arms had transformed into branches with twig-like fingers that stretched out. Living ivy grew over the statue, covering most of her face, the top of her breasts, and reaching between her legs like shadows. The living ivy had wound itself round the stone leaves.

The name of the sculptor had been engraved in small but clear lettering on one of the roots: Edward Melfort. Edward leant down and read out loud to Iris the inscription on the pedestal:

46

It is for love I pursue you. You make me miserable,
for fear you should fall and hurt yourself on these
stones and I should be the cause.

'Who said that?' Iris asked.

'Apollo. As she ran from him, Daphne pleaded with her father, the river god, to be turned into a tree rather than be raped by Apollo.'

Listening to Edward, Iris recognized the expressionless quality that permeated the painting of his family. Edward had at first seemed very different from Louis, but she was beginning now to recognize an introverted nature which belonged to both brothers. Whether this was to do with their dominant mother, the war, or perhaps with Daphne's death, she was not sure.

'But your name is from Greek mythology, isn't it?' Edward said. 'Iris was the rainbow and messenger of the gods. She was sent to wake up Morpheus.' He looked at her with eagle eyes. 'I wonder what kind of sculpture *you* would make? Let me see you in profile.'

As he roughly turned her around it seemed that he overshadowed her with overpowering wings, and she instinctively pushed him away.

'I'm sorry,' he said, swiftly transforming back into his previous character.

Relenting, Iris said, 'You can sculpt me if you want.'

She knew it would be an opportunity to find out more about Daphne. There was another reason for accepting his offer that she could not yet admit to herself.

Edward bowed down low in mocking gratitude.

Iris was convinced that the falconer knew why her sister had taken her life. However, she thought Hector must have been wrong when he had talked of the falconer's infatuation with Daphne. The falconer was not a man interested in love. The falconer's passion for his work seemed to exclude any other kind of desire, and nor did he have the ways of a man used to women.

In the company of Iris and Muriel, the falconer pushed out his arm as a signal for the falcon to take off, and she flew up into the sky with a rapid beat of its wings.

The bird hovered between the sky and the top of the fog. She was threatening to dive down out of sight into the grey fog. The falconer signalled to Muriel. She put out her arm, a chunk of rabbit in her hand, and the bird swooped down, her wings huge and looming, and landed on her outstretched hand. The bird rotated her head, her eyes flashing.

Muriel then proceeded to help the falconer weigh the other birds in the caged baskets, to check they were not too heavy. The birds had to be hungry before they left, and below a certain weight or they would not bother to return. This is what it is like with Muriel, Iris realized – the falconer keeps her hungry for his attention and she keeps on returning.

The falconer's face seemed darker today. His black hair seemed lighter, the colour of a buzzard's brown wing. His grey eyes were like ash. There was something slightly frightening about him, as if he were a pent-up force, ready to take off into the sky. The birds were his desires unleashed, the flight of birds a projection of his thoughts. And he had such power over the birds that they obeyed his every command. As did Muriel. He treated Muriel like he treated his birds – as an extension of his wishes, Iris thought. Muriel, who seemed such an unpredictable spirit, obeyed every nod, every gesture of his hand.

And Iris wondered what Lady Melfort thought about Muriel's devotion to the falconer. She probably didn't concern herself, she probably didn't even want to know. Almain Castle didn't seem to be a place of familial love. But Iris found the power he had over the girl deeply threatening.

Muriel was overtaken by her passion for the falconer. She dreamt of becoming his falcon, of his gauntleted hand. She dreamt of wheeling in the sky and seeing him below, amongst the lines and diagonals of fields and rivers. And the feeling

48

of the breeze against her wings, and the sun beating down as she flew up toward it, was akin to the love she felt for the falconer.

No longer earthbound, she was as light as the air itself. She could dance in the sky. She had found grace at last. It was what she had been looking for.

Chapter 10

One morning, Iris overheard Lord and Lady Melfort's raised voices in the drawing room. Checking that nobody was watching her, Iris stayed to listen at the door. She heard Lady Melfort saying to her husband in her cold dogmatic voice, 'The more I read what you bring me, the more I find their ideas distasteful. The Nazis are full of contradictions. Herr Hitler loves to say that he "thinks with his blood." He boasts of Germany's romantic neopaganism, her worship of forests and nature and strange beasts. Yet their dogma is rigid and ideological, their horrible architecture full of straight lines. National Socialism is profoundly *unnatural*. Instinct and reason, reason and instinct. They are false opposites. We live with them both. We should deny *neither*. You choose to ignore these contradictions, which cause such sickness to Germany, Xavier. It has become a diseased country.'

Iris heard her husband try to reply, in his customary soft and conciliatory manner.

The end of May was humid; after days of rain the temperature suddenly soared, and the resulting mist bathed the mountains in diffuse smoke. Layers of pale light threaded through the morning sky, outlining the grey clouds in gold. Heat and dampness were written all over the sky. The urgency of growth seemed hallucinatory, the buds of the silver birch springing up like small candles and the ferns, yellow lurid green, unfurling as if visibly before her eyes. Even the singing of the birds quickened, the notes coming out shallow and fast.

One morning, Iris decided to follow the stony path that

led behind the castle up the mountains. As she picked her way through a particularly woody area, a huge stag suddenly ran across her path. Seeing her, he immediately stopped and stared at her with huge limpid eyes, his antlers branching out into the sky. The intensity of his gaze stopped her heart. She felt as if she were looking through time. The stag darted off through the trees and she ran after him, as if compelled by a spell he had cast on her.

But as she ran, the clammy air seemed to stifle the air she breathed and made the burgeoning life around her increasingly unnatural. Sweat was pouring down her face and she was finding it difficult to breathe. Her armpits and her back grew wet.

She kept catching russet glimmers of the stag through the trees, always just a little ahead of her. It was leading her up the mountain. As she climbed higher, the grass grew thicker and greener, and reeds began to pierce the tullochs with cotton tufts, white as Coll's hair. The ruins of deserted estate cottages were scattered around her. She became vaguely aware of the ground growing softer beneath her shoes. The swampy earth was now sucking in her feet, making it increasingly difficult to walk – but she persevered, determined not to lose sight of the magnificent animal.

The stag reached the summit and finally ran off, leaving Iris high above the glen. To her horror, Iris saw what the stag had led her to: in the distance, a disembodied head seemed to be lying in the centre of a bog. Cassie was running around it, frantically yelping. But as Iris grew nearer she could see it was Coll, buried up to his neck in mud, on the verge of sinking completely beneath it.

She had to help him. Without thinking of her own safety, she began to drag a large branch across the bog towards him. The boggy ground was turning into mud that now reached up to her thighs. Still she went on, pulling her dress up to her waist. She only stopped when her legs had become completely trapped in the thick intransigent mud. She could go no further. Iris flung the branch toward him.

'Hold onto the other end, Coll,' she shouted to him and, inch by muddy inch, Iris pulled him out, until he lay exhausted beside her on the firmer ground. His mud-saturated body made him look as if he had been earth-born. The dog, her thin urgent body panting beneath her black and white silky coat, ran around Coll's mud-caked body excitedly, as if she had discovered a new creature.

The boy was in a state of shock, and Iris gently led him to a nearby stream where she helped wash the mud off his arms and legs. As she splashed the cold water over him she felt an affinity with the boy: they had both lost their mothers young. Her own mother had taken her life soon after Daphne had been born. She also felt a strange new aching caring, and wondered if this was the feeling that mothers had for their sons.

Silently, Coll undid the laces of Iris's shoes and took them off her feet. He sat down on a nearby rock, took a knife from one of his pockets, and began scraping the mud off their soles. Sunlight glinted on a gold charm hanging from a chain on his neck. It was an emblem of an eagle perched on a swastika, smattered with mud, which the water had only partially cleaned.

'Who gave you that?' she asked.

Coll at once turned sullen and uncooperative, and his body hunched slightly, as if shielding the question. He dropped her shoes to the ground.

'I didn't steal it.' he said defensively.

'I wasn't suggesting that.'

'Daphne gave it to me.'

She wondered where Daphne had got it from. Daphne had never been interested in politics.

'The lady who was killed by the beast,' the boy continued.

Iris felt shocked and angry. 'You mean by the mythical beast in the forest? There's no such thing, Coll. If there *is* an animal it will probably be a black panther, escaped from the zoo.'

52

His pale eyes seemed to open up at wonderment at her stupidity.

'What will make you believe me?' he asked, and without waiting for the answer, took off down the hill, his dog by his side.

He had found her body decomposing under one of the trees in the petrified forest. He knew it was where the beast kept its lair. She had been curled up under a tree, her bones as white as the stone trees.

A Red Admiral butterfly flickered among the tall grasses; the heat brought out a sweetness in the air. The day seemed to be humming at a low frequency. It was still quite early, the sun beginning its slow ascent towards noon.

The falconer withdrew into his room, and as he shut the door on the light, a cool melancholy swept over it like the shadow of a bird's wing. His room was small and dark. It had a smell of must and damp which Iris found comforting, like rotting autumnal leaves. A china dog sat on the mantelpiece and a rush mat lined the floor. His bothy was down the road from the old schoolhouse. He kept his peregrine falcon in his cottage, and his hawks and eagle in the mews.

Iris watched from a chair as the falconer put a saucepan of water on the fire for tea. He sat down opposite her and emptied his mind of thoughts. He would often do that. Just sit, his mind empty like an empty vase. He could pass the time for hours like this. Other people could flicker in and out of the space around him like fireflies in the darkness.

His hand was trembling from this solitary summer. A strong hand shaking through the effort of restraining hidden thoughts. His strong hand that was fragile because it was made of skin and bone, whereas these thoughts were cruel and limitless. But it is flesh that, in the end, will out. He would put his omnipotent thoughts out into the ether, along with the mosquitoes and dust motes.

He extended his arm. The peregrine flew from its perch in

53

the corner of the room and settled onto it. She crouched on his gauntlet, her round yellow eyes with dilated pupils, full of nothing but instinctive will. Her wire claws clutched onto his thick leather gauntlet. The bird's feathery legs bloomed out like little pantaloons. Her head was still and her small pointed beak looked merciless.

Iris watched him stroke the warm, breathing bulk of the falcon's body with his left ungloved hand. Only her feathers were redolent of softness, lying in staggered layers along her closed wings. Her breast was white and soft, downy with smaller feathers. The wings were myriad shades of brown and black, the same subtle tones as the fauna of the countryside.

The falcon turned her head around and gave her master an impassive look.

'Even after all these years, it's difficult to read their minds,' he said. He stared at Iris for a moment. 'Like yours.'

'What do you mean?'

'Drummond isn't your real name, is it?'

Iris knew it would be foolish to show any vulnerability to the falconer.

'I doubt they would have given me the job if I had told them my real name. But how did you guess?'

He laughed. 'You have the same look in your eyes as hers, sometimes. But don't worry. We all have secrets here.'

'Edward mentioned she was acting strangely before she died.'

The falconer hesitated, then said, 'She became convinced something was following her.'

'People talk about a beast,' she said, sardonically.

'The beast of Glen Almain is supposed to be half-human, half-beast. Daphne kept dreaming he was waiting for her in the petrified forest.'

'What supernatural nonsense!'

'Daphne would hear howling outside her window at night. She was sure the beast had left the glen and come into the castle's garden. She never saw it. But she said it followed her when she walked in the glen. In the last few days, she refused to leave her room at all.'

'And the beast is part of the glen's folklore?'

He looked at her amused. 'Oh, no. He's the beast in all of us. The part of nature in us we like to hide. The beast's as real as you or I.'

That night, Iris dreamt that the beast was somewhere outside, beyond the garden. The moon was pendulous in the sky, slightly pink, flushed in its swollen state. It was low in the sky too, weighed down by its fullness. It looked as if it were made of flesh. The beast's howl was bewitching. She tossed and turned in her bed, the heavy cotton sheets lying cold and damp on her. Heavy as the moon. Her body felt hot and feverish as the tree outside the window scratched at the pane absent-mindedly.

The howling shivered through her body, as if it were not the beast that were crying out, but herself. She felt possessed, her body wracked by the sound. She became confused in her half-sleeping state – was she the beast, or the beast her? She dreamt she was running through the forest, panting, her mouth full of the taste of blood, weighed down by her new animal nature and the full moon.

Chapter 11

The following evening, Iris took a walk amongst the sloping fields of meadowsweet, shepherd's-purse and delicate ragged robin. How could Daphne have killed herself in such a place? Iris did not believe in the existence of a beast, but knew there had to be a reason for her sister's descent into paranoia – a reason hard as the granite rock of the mountains. The answer was somewhere in the glen, she knew that. Somewhere amongst its streams and pools and mountains.

A soft breeze started up amongst the trees above her, as if the glen was whispering to her the answer in the language of leaves. The mountains were clothed in a haze, the fir trees rising out like phantom trees. The sky was lilac, tinged with the pink of the sunset hidden behind the hills. The landscape was textured soft, and the lines of the hills smudged like pencil.

And here was her sister, rising out from this backdrop of mother-of-pearl light. Her hair was a vapour of light around her porcelain face. Iris walked towards the vision of Daphne and put her arms around her body as she dissolved into the mist.

The falconer's appearance seemed as transient as the weather; one moment his crooked back almost disappearing, another moment growing more prominent. She watched the hawk circle above his head; his leather gauntlet was stained with the blood of raw meat. She focused on the light that fell on the fool's gold of a nearby rock. The trickle of a stream was like the music that fairies might have made, as mist hovered over the mountains. The landscape looked tenuous, as if it were a part of fairyland.

'I'm seeing apparitions of my sister in the glen,' she said to him.

'Perhaps it's Queen Mab of the fairies.'

His soft voice, husky, easily lost in the wind, was soporific. He probably used it as a charm, she thought, to bewitch the birds, to make cooing sounds, cries of attack and to sing paeans of seduction.

'Who's Queen Mab?'

'She's the fairies' midwife – employed by the fairies to deliver our minds of dreams.'

'It does look like fairies could live here, running over the rocks.'

The falconer, still keeping his eye on the bird, replied, 'The glen has always been inhabited. You can see them at twilight.'

The falconer watched the bird hover above the warm currents of the air. 'The fairies are more an effect, a shower of impressions: quicksilver movements, sunlight on water.'

His eyes were so hard, she thought, like the eyes of a hawk. And yet he talks of a mystical beast, and of a Queen Mab. What was strange about the falconer, she was beginning to realize, was that although he acted in the most pragmatic of ways, he said fanciful things. He typified the contradictory qualities of men and women: the most rational could be the most theoretical, the cruelest the most prone to sentimental fancies. And didn't his birds, who hunted so mercilessly, fly in the air like archangels?

You, Iris, the fairies whispered, will go through the glen, trampling over us, treading over our paths, oblivious to our presence. But we will leave traces of wetness and dark red clay, fern pollen and blue petal on your skin, as marks of our presence. As we once did on your sister.

Edward's studio was in the servant's quarters at the back of the castle, down a narrow dark corridor. Unlike the small basic rooms that the domestic servants slept in, his light-filled studio was large and roomy, with French doors that opened up onto a back courtyard. Huge canvases were propped up against the walls. Clay-covered tools were scattered over the wooden floor, smattered in clay dust and old paint. A moth-eaten blue velvet chair stood in the centre of the room; he motioned Iris to sit in it, so that he could sculpt her head.

He stared at her hard before moulding the clay with his fingers, dabbing, prodding and pressing. He was dealing in wet earth. She felt uncomfortable, as if he were pressing her own face beneath his fingers. He would look up once or twice at her, and then seem to forget her as he concentrated on the clay head, his fingers wet and sticky with the clay.

'Your mother told me how much the war has changed Louis,' she said quietly, after he had been working in silence for a while.

'He's like a changeling. He still sees terrible things. The violence and horror. The images have never left him. To look at him you would think he sees the glen – but he sees other things instead.'

'What happened to him during the war?'

'No-one knows. He has never spoken of it. But that's why my mother seems so hard. It's a shell.'

'Only a shell?' Iris asked.

Edward hesitated. 'At first. But I think now she has become her shell. That's what happens sometimes. A shell starts off as protection for the inner self, but then the inner self calcifies too. Don't go looking for any fragility beneath her surface – there's none left. She's no time for understanding others, and least of all for understanding herself.'

In the light Edward looked petrified himself, his whole face immobile. All expression had left him, and Iris wondered if he was really talking about himself.

Edward's independence, underneath his charm, was extreme and unassailable and built on a fear of love. Women were magical creatures, but they could also wield terrible power and, like the Medusa, turn men into stone. He could not risk love. Daphne had been the exception. And he had lost her. And he would never be allowed to talk of it.

Shifting the subject abruptly, he asked, 'Do you want to take a look?'

She rose from the chair and came round to the plinth where he had been working. There was only a rough outline, but she recognized something in the face that belonged to her: her concentrated nature.

'So, Louis is the reason why your mother collects paintings of dead children?'

For a moment Edward's face turned to stone with grief.

'No', he replied. 'Not for that reason.'

After a few more minutes, he stood up and went to the small sink in the corner of the room and washed his hands. He then put a moist cloth over the clay head. All without saying anything. Then he turned and walked up to her chair and, looking down, traced the silhouette of her face with his damp clean finger. She tried not to tremble under his touch.

'Yes,' he said. 'A strong face. You are very deceptive, Iris. Very quiet and observant, but all the time thinking and plotting away. You should be careful: my mother doesn't like cuckoos in her nest.'

As she returned to her room from Edward's studio, Iris was walking down one of the corridors when she heard singing coming from another part of the castle. It seemed to be emanating from the East Wing. A woman's voice. She thought at first it might belong to Muriel, but the voice seemed too full of depth for her girlish tones. The singer seemed in absolute control of her medium. Like a siren's song, it seemed to be luring Iris to one of the unexplored rooms adjacent to Daphne's room. But when she knocked on the door, the singing abruptly stopped and there was no

59

further reply.

The following day Louis stopped her in the corridor, looking excited and nervous. 'The estate workers' summer dance is this evening. Would you care to join me?' he asked abruptly. Louis' gaucheness, she now realized, was part of the damage that the war had done to him. She felt keenly the importance of getting to know both brothers.

'I'll meet you there,' she said, and Louis gave her a broad Cheshire cat grin.

In a cream cotton dress and sandals, she walked the mile to the complex of cottages and warehouses at the edge of the estate. Louis was waiting for her at the entrance of the barn, wearing a pale linen suit which emphasized his fragile frame.

Inside, the energy of the barn was invigorating. The barn's cold stone walls were sweating with heat from the dancing bodies, and the straw on the flagstone floor was wet with spilt beer. Empty barrels had been upturned for tables and chairs. The laughter and the noise of the reels created a joyous, manic atmosphere, the revellers acting as though possessed.

Iris and Louis stood by the wall for a while, watching the dancing. Hector was standing in one corner with one of the parlour maids, a particularly beautiful girl with copper hair.

'Hector looks like an Aryan superman, doesn't he?' Iris shouted over the music.

'I wouldn't be surprised if he made sacrifices to a pagan god,' Louis replied. Iris laughed.

Louis brought a drink over to her and said matter-of-factly, 'I took Daphne Tennant to a dance here, too.'

'Do you make a habit of taking your father's secretaries to dances?' she asked, flippantly.

'Only if they're interesting.' He clings to his intelligence like a man clinging to a rock, Iris thought.

'Dance with me, Iris,' Louis said, and his hand languidly took hers as if it were made neither of flesh nor blood. She smiled at him, but he seemed preoccupied – as if he was hardly aware she was there. Her presence had become as tenuous as his.

He led her on to the uneven floor of the barn. Louis' dancing seemed half-fluent, half-jerky, like a puppet whose strings had been loosened. They danced the reels together as if they were strangers. Only when the sweat was pouring down their backs did they stop. They stood silent and still in the centre of the barn while the fiddlers continued to play and the dancers cavorted around them.

The following morning, Iris looked out of her window and saw Hector disappear through the entrance of the circular yew hedge that surrounded a statue of Apollo. A few minutes later, she watched Lady Melfort walk down the path towards the same hedge and vanish behind it. She waited for them to reappear. She waited for a while.

Iris put on a light jacket and walked out into the garden. She followed the path that they had taken down to the hedge, trying to tread as softly as she could on the loose gravel. The head of Apollo, god of the sun, was peeping over the top of the perfectly trimmed hedge.

Inexorably, she drew nearer. She could hear hushed, intimate whispers and then clearly the words, 'Daphne came between us,' spoken by Lady Melfort. Iris was on the other side of the hedge from them now, a slight breeze caressing her cheek. Between a gap in the leaves she could see that Hector and Margaret Melfort were kissing.

'Why hallo, Iris.' A deep voice sounded behind her. Startled, she turned round; Lord Melfort had silently walked up behind her.

He seemed to be charmingly innocuous, deflecting attention away from himself just by the way he was standing, as if any meaning she imparted to him would refract off him like sunlight on metal. And she would be blinded by her own view of him.

'What are you doing, lurking around in the garden?

61

Shouldn't you be in the library?' His words sounded stern, but his blue eyes looked benignly amused.

'I felt like some fresh air,' she said, with some hesitation.

'Yes, the library does grow a bit fusty after a while.' He paused for a moment. 'You haven't seen my wife, by any chance, have you? Mrs Elliot said she was in the garden, but she doesn't seem to be here, after all.'

A silence emanated from behind the hedge, and Iris suppressed a hysterical urge to laugh. She looked down at the ground. 'I'd better return to the library,' she said. 'Do some work, before lunch.'

She met his eyes, but couldn't read the look in them. He does this deliberately, she thought; somehow he manages to have this effect. She did not know why he did this – to what ends – but it prevented a reading of him that was anything but subjective or imaginary.

She wondered if he would walk back with her, but he didn't. He walked on, past the hedge, toward the greenhouse. He suspects, she thought – more: under his urbane, detached manner he knows about his wife. Iris was shocked by Lady Melfort's betrayal of her husband. But then, Hector was more a manifestation of nature than a man – it would have been difficult to resist him.

The mutability of the glen was bewitching her. It was never the same; from minute to minute there were changes in the light, the temperature, the colour of things. It was constantly shifting and it made her feel that she herself was transforming.

Iris walked down the glen and saw Muriel coming up from the river, carrying a fishing-rod over her shoulder.

'I never see you studying. Shouldn't you be doing some school work?' Iris asked.

'Soon I will be sixteen,' Muriel said. 'And then no-one will be able to tell me what to do. I shall be all grown-up and haughty.'

Iris laughed. 'Are you sure that's what you want?'

Muriel smiled, 'I would rather die!'

A slight drizzle was alighting on Muriel's cropped hair, like a sprinkling of little glass beads. Her cheeks were flushed from exertion and the cool damp air. Her dark hair had curled up in the rain.

'I've heard singing,' Iris said. 'Coming from the East Wing. Is there another woman staying in the castle? Someone I've never met?'

The girl looked so fey, Iris thought, with her dark eyes that stared out of her cat-like face. Looking at Muriel made trying to focus on anything else very difficult. It was impossible to concentrate on her fully, for her looks always pulled the watcher away, like a magician distracting with one hand what was really happening with the other.

In youth, it was far easier to be different from how one looked, Iris thought. As one grew older, the face and the soul came together; the clues to character became mapped out on the skin. The inside and outside met in the set of the face and the way the lips drew together. But none of this had happened to Muriel yet. She was still in disguise.

'That's Agnes. It's not surprising you haven't met her yet: she never leaves her room. She has agoraphobia. All she can do is sing, read and look after her birds.'

'And who is Agnes?'

'Agnes is Mummy's younger sister. But they don't talk to each other any more.'

'Why not?'

'Oh, Mummy thinks she's wanting to cause trouble for the family.'

'How?'

'Daddy's work is top secret…' Muriel trailed off. The girl was looking at Iris hard, as if thinking ahead in a long intricate line of twisting possibilities. As if she calculated other people's responses. 'But you had a younger sister too…'

'The falconer told you?'

'Don't worry. We won't tell anyone else.'

Muriel hesitated a moment, before adding, 'I really don't

know what happened to Daphne, Iris. I sometimes think everyone knows what happened that night except Coll and me. But I did hear voices coming from her room on the evening she died. I heard her say clearly, 'Please, stop me going into the forest.' A man then replied, but I couldn't hear what he said.'

'Did you recognize his voice?'

'He sounded foreign.'

On returning to the library that afternoon, Iris passed a type of file she hadn't seen before, lying on Lord Melfort's desk. The document was marked in red ink, MOST SECRET: *Biological Warfare Tests: Recent Results from Gruinard Island.* She opened it up, her eyes darting quickly over the words: *Bacillus Anthracis.* She heard footsteps outside, and quickly returned to her desk before Lord Melfort came in.

At night, Iris heard the howling call out to her again, as if drawing her outside. She went downstairs into the garden. Peering into the darkness, she saw something move about between the hedges. She let out a cry, but it was only Coll who suddenly appeared in front of her.

'You gave me a fright!' The boy's eyes looked so large and pale in the moonlight. His dog was barking frantically at his side.

'She's been like this for hours. She's gone quite mad,' Coll said. For a moment, he looked like a child lost in the forest of his thoughts, tripping up on roots of unpalatable events. He bent down and stroked the dog's back, but Cassie refused to be calmed. The boy was perturbed. They shared a certain state of mind, and if one was disturbed, so was the other.

'Go home,' Iris told the boy gently, and Coll led Cassie, still barking, back towards the avenue, only stopping for a moment to pick up a wounded blackbird that lay on the ground. Iris was left alone in the garden.

Something was moving in the shadows far off, where the garden met the wildness. At first it looked human, but then she realized it must be a huge animal of some kind, hunched and obscure. It merged with the shadows and disappeared into the recesses of the trees, as if not made of flesh and bone but of atoms of darkness formed from the blackness of night.

Stars scattered over the sky like frozen points of ice. The new moon was sharp and pointed at the tips of its scimitar curve. It was such a still night – as if the world had been fashioned from glass. The night air was cold enough to catch her breath. Iris touched her face. She too felt as if she were made of glass, and that if she were to turn and take the first step back to the castle, she might shatter into pieces. So she stood still in the moonlight, waiting, waiting to see a glimpse of what she had seen again but there was nothing, only the glimmer of leaves.

That night, Iris dreamt Daphne was crossing the field of the small island of Gruinard, which lay edged with rocks in the middle of a stormy sea. The field was littered with huddled bodies. At first Iris thought they were sheep, but as she looked more closely at the hunched shapes scattered over the fields, she saw that they were not animals at all, but dead soldiers.

Chapter 12

The following morning, Iris noticed Coll walking down the glen road towards her. Instead of being lost in his own world as usual, he was looking anxiously all around him. She felt there was something missing and then she realized what it was – he was without his dog.

'You've lost Cassie?'

He nodded. 'Last night, I left Cassie in the outdoor kennel of the old schoolhouse. The next morning she'd gone. Someone had unchained her.'

His eyes began to fill with tears, and as she put an arm around him she could feel him give in to her, his sense of loss making him forget himself. He had the burnt toast smell of boy.

She surveyed the landscape for the dog. It was easy to see something shift in the open landscape. A moving deer, even camouflaged, was conspicuous a mile away. This was how hawks saw their prey, she thought – the eye could catch motion. But she could not see the black and white motion that was Cassie.

That night Iris, on retiring to bed, heard a rustle. She sat up, and saw a note being slipped under her bedroom door. She rushed to open the door and stared down the darkening corridor. The back of a willowy woman dressed in a long cream silk gown disappeared round the corner, her diaphanous dress fluttering like the wings of an owl. She was sure it was Agnes. But how had she managed to leave her room? Iris returned to her room; she picked up the note and read,

And 'mid these dancing rocks at once and ever
It flung up momently the sacred river.
Five miles meandering with a mazy motion
Through wood and dale the sacred river ran,
Then reached the caverns measureless to man,
And sank in tumult to a lifeless ocean:
And 'mid this tumult Kubla heard from far
Ancestral voices prophesying war!

Why had Agnes given her a poem prophesying a war? There could *not* be another war – not after so many years of peace. It was against all reason.

Over the following days as Iris, Coll and some of the estate workers looked for Cassie, an irascible summer wind blew up. Birds could not fly where they liked in the open sky. Clouds moved too fast for comfort. Iris felt that the glen was looking for the dog, shaking its own veneer, looking behind the hawthorn bushes and between the long grasses. The hot wind left the searchers' equilibrium disturbed. The wind blew through their emotions, shaking them as it did the branches of the trees. They found themselves unaccountably more impatient, unpredictable, more prone to gusts of anger.

Gradually, one by one, the estate workers, farmers and shepherds returned to their work, mending fences, rounding up sheep and digging ditches, as if everything had gone back to normal.

One late afternoon, Coll came up to Iris in the avenue. 'Please come with me, Iris.'

He took her hand and led her down to the river at the bottom of the glen and over the iron bridge. The boy then pointed to bloody marks that smeared the grass: old blood, the colour of rust. Iris followed the traces. At the entrance to the petrified forest lay a bone, like a small child's arm.

'Stay here,' Iris said to Coll, who stood shivering a few feet behind. Iris entered the forest. The air was very still; she noticed a pungent smell like wild garlic, potent but sensual.

She followed the scent. She came to more bones, bones that had been heaped into a pile, and then saw what looked like heart-shaped prints, bigger than a sheep or a deer, in the damp earth beneath the trees. She began to follow them.

The sun was disappearing beneath the horizon. There was now that odd light – the light that happens when the sun is going down but there is still a white sky above and the trees are silhouetted against the sky. As if the earth has turned dark, away from the sun, but the trees are still miraculously shining.

Under the stone roots of one of the petrified trees lay the carcass of a dog. The remaining skeleton looked like part of a fallen tree. Flies were buzzing around the morass of flesh. There seemed only to be a pulpy mass of fat and skin and a smell of decaying flesh that permeated the air.

Iris tried to pull her gaze away, yet she found the repulsiveness of what she saw compelling, as if by staring at it she could in some way begin to understand something at the fringes of her consciousness. She felt the presence of some animate thing between the trees. Unthinkingly, she looked around, but could see nothing. The pale sky above the outline of the bare trees looked dull, a monotonous light that had no dimension to it. This was a dead place.

She returned to the edge of the wood, where the boy was still waiting. How was she to tell the boy about the dog – what had happened to her, where she now lay? She knew how much Cassie had meant to the boy. And she knew that grief would prostrate him.

'There's no need to go into the wood,' was all she could say, gently.

Coll looked into her eyes and understood what she had seen. He nodded blankly, as his eyes filled with tears.

'Hector always knows when it's time.'

'Time for what?'

'Time for another sacrifice to the beast.'

'What are you talking about, Coll? There is no beast. It's just local superstition. It was probably some wild animal

68

who killed Cassie,' she said emphatically. She still couldn't accept its reality.

He looked at her, his face now full of bitter uncaring. 'Daphne too, was a sacrifice. Just like Cassie. *Now* do you believe me about the beast?'

'You're being absurd.'

'They let Daphne go into the wood. *They did nothing to help her.*'

'Coll, *it was just a bad dream.*'

It was late at night, and the doors that lined the long corridor of the East Wing were making Iris feel uneasy, as if a stranger lurked behind each one. The ethereal singing was leading her back; the fluctuating light of the lamps threw looming shadows over the walls. This time, when she knocked on the door, a voice said, 'Come in.'

Iris opened the door. Toys were scattered over the bare floorboards – a spinning top, a terrier dog on wheels with stuffing coming out of its back. It was a child's nursery. Stencils of boats had been drawn around the walls.

A woman in her late fifties was sitting at a table, tending to an injured blackbird. Beside the blackbird on the table were piles of papers covered in what appeared to be hieroglyphics.

Agnes had very large eyes, like a nocturnal creature. An owl, Iris thought. The eyes seemed round and black and all-seeing at the same time. The paleness of her face and hair made her look as if she came from the petrified forest: her hair had the silver look of the stone trees. There was something about her that reminded Iris of Muriel. Muriel's otherworldliness seemed to have come from her aunt.

Agnes was smiling slightly.

'This used to be a child's room,' Iris said.

'Yes,' Agnes said. 'It was the Melfort children's nursery. What can I do for you?'

Iris wasn't sure what this woman could do for her. 'I'm working for Lord Melfort.'

69

'Ah, for Xavier. Idealists are dangerous men.'

'But his ideals are honourable.'

'That doesn't mean he isn't dangerous.' She looked at Iris thoughtfully. 'Iris – the messenger of the gods. I've been waiting for you. I have to do a lot of waiting. It's so frustrating not being able to leave this room.'

Agnes' face reminded Iris of a mask, as if a piece of exquisite ivory had been placed over her face and only those dark owl eyes were expressive of who she was.

'So how did you deliver the poem? I saw you walking down the corridor.'

Agnes laughed. 'Oh, *that* was magic. That particular spell only works once.'

'What a pity,' Iris said, ironically.

The blackbird emitted a squeak. Ignoring Iris' tone, Agnes began bandaging its wing. 'Some people think of birds as evil spirits that flutter through the mind, their evil thoughts mirrored in these creatures' jerky flights,' she said in her resonant, musical voice. 'They seem to undermine the *status quo*. Crows especially are seen as evil. But sometimes I see them sliding down a snow-covered roof, for fun. And once some beakers were left out and I watched one of them stack a tower with them. Crows are playful and smart birds.'

'Did Coll bring you the blackbird?'

She nodded. 'Even Xavier himself once brought me a bird with a broken leg.'

Agnes was beginning to give off a potent energy. It was as if her aura was spreading all over the room. The objects in the room – the rocking horse, the jack-in-the-box, and the sharp-edged tin cars with their missing wheels – were all becoming part of her. They were where the hard parts of her body stuck out. The room seemed to have become a fabrication of her bones and her waking consciousness.

Agnes stood up from the table and walked over to the window that overlooked the balcony. When she moved she became very supple and fluid, as if she were made of water. She crossed the room as if flowing from one place to another, never quite leaving one place before she reached the other. Her fluidity lent her a silvery vital spirit.

A bird table made of pale oak studded with semi-precious stones glimmered on the balcony. In the moonlight the amethyst, moonstone and topaz glittered.

'I had this table made to attract the bird of paradise. It loves glistening things,' Agnes said. 'I know one day I will spot him. He might even come to my window. That's what I live for. The day that he will come.'

One late afternoon, Louis and Iris were watching the minnows darting about in the pool's amber water. 'The pool was her favourite place,' Louis said. 'Daphne would stand there' – and he pointed to the same spot amongst the reeds where Iris liked to stand – 'and just watch the water and listen to the sound of the waterfall. She loved late afternoon, just before dusk. She said it reminded her of how to feel.'

Iris remembered how Coll had thought this place was haunted. Louis still didn't know who she was, she realized.

'You, Iris, are beginning to feel, aren't you? Glen Almain is a place of change, of metamorphosis.'

Louis took her hand and led her over some stepping stones to the back of the waterfall. A wide ledge of stone had formed behind the cataract to create a hall of green glass. The water gushed over them in an arc. The noise was tremendous, blocking out all thoughts.

As she stood beside him she began to feel enchanted, as if inevitably reminded of who she was. And, of all sensations, this one was the most powerfully seductive, for it was not simply a matter of desire but of her shrouded heart. She felt as if, like a magpie, Louis were stealing emotion from her heart.

The evening light shone down through the glasshouse of water. The setting sun was far above, and below it Louis looked avenging. The war had marked his eyes. Suddenly, she wanted to laugh – at the absurdity and inevitability of what she was about to do. She put up her arms and brought his

71

head down to kiss him. The kiss was mechanical. He is like a wound-up doll, she thought. A shadow crossed her heart. 'You're like the other side of her,' he whispered.

The following week, Iris knocked on Louis' door. They had not talked properly since their kiss beneath the waterfall. Louis' tired pale face seemed to her empty of everything but an essential spirit. As if he had been shorn even further of physical presence and his body replaced by this thin wraith.

Tapestries depicting the myth of Diana and Actaeon ran along the frieze of the wall. In mushroom and pinks, the images seemed to weigh the room down. Diana bathing naked, Actaeon spying on her, Actaeon turning into a deer and being hunted by her, and Actaeon being torn to pieces by her hounds. Iris remembered Edward spying on her as she bathed. Outside the window, Iris could see the tawny gold mountains covered by the dark woods. Here, in this room, was another petrified place.

'This is your sanctuary.'

He shrugged his shoulders. He looks like one of his relics, she thought: *if I touched him he would turn to dust.* She wondered about the locked drawer in the cabinet, its walnut sheen glistening like spilt blood, its ivory handles like bone.

'What was war like, Louis?'

He looked at her. 'At the Somme, it is said we were like *"mischievous apes tearing up the image of God."'*

'But here you're safe.'

'The glen's full of beasts.'

'I thought there was only one,' she said, ironically. 'The beast of Glen Almain. You have one of his teeth in your drawers.'

He traced the faint lines around her eyes. 'I mean the beasts in human form.'

She needed to open that drawer.

'Louis, I'm feeling faint. Would you mind fetching me a drink?'

72

He leaned forward and kissed her. His lips were dry and immaculate. 'I'll fetch you a glass of water from the kitchen.'

As soon as Louis had left the room, Iris hurried over to the Glen Almain cabinet. She opened the glass door, tried the drawer – it was still locked. Where would he have hidden the key? Acting from instinct, she lifted up the amber paperweight on the nearby shelf: *May your dreams come true.* Underneath lay the small key she had been looking for.

She opened the drawer and saw tiny shards of animal bone lying inside: *from the antler of a roe deer, from the collarbone of a hare.* The bone of a finger also lay there and, picking it up with a shaking hand, she read the label: *Daphne's finger, left behind by the beast of Glen Almain.* The blood sang in her ears. She let the bone drop back into the drawer. Next to the finger lay a faded envelope, marked *Daphne's suicide letter.* Before she had time to pick it up, Louis' footsteps sounded in the corridor, and she quickly shut the drawer again, turning the key and closing the glass doors.

Louis came in, holding a glass of water, and saw her standing by the bureau.

'Do you feel better now?'

She nodded. Louis put the glass down and walked up to her, binding her to him with strong, thin arms like wire.

The gardens looked almost two dimensional in the heat when finally she managed to escape from Louis' room. As she walked about the formal gardens, the statues watched her like silent witnesses. Unease began to accompany her like the lengthening shadows. A sense of discomfort followed her like the breeze blowing through the trees. She came to standstill. For a moment, she felt unable to move – she had become as inanimate as stone. Suddenly, she had entered a dimension where there was no sound and no shadows. There was no past, no future – only an eternal present.

A few days later, Iris was tidying Lord Melfort's desk in the library when she noticed that another confidential file had been left open by his inkwell. The lower half of the page was covered in mathematical formulas, like arcane spells. She heard footsteps outside the library door and closed the file, returning to her desk as Louis came in. Since her discovery of the cabinet's contents, he now disturbed her deeply and she had begun to avoid him.

'Louis, why are you following me?'

He smiled at her. 'It may seem as if I'm following you. But it's just a coincidence.'

She must have looked flustered, and his gaze immediately fell onto the confidential file on the desk.

'Snooping around, Iris? If it's to do with my father, you're playing with fire. Why do you think he leaves these confidential files lying around?'

'Please leave me alone.'

'Iris, I am not following you around! It's your imagination. I wanted to return a book.' He held it up.

She flounced out of the library and down the hall. She half-expected him to follow her, but when she turned to see if he were, he was walking in the opposite direction towards the dining room, his graceful, loping body moving away from her.

She turned and walked swiftly back to the library. She opened the file on Lord Melfort's desk, and began flicking through its pages. A passage heavily annotated in dark green ink caught her eye:

> If bacteria are inhaled, symptoms develop in two or three days. Initial symptoms resemble common respiratory infection but are followed by high fever, joint ache and laboured breathing. Internal bleeding is followed by external black lesions.

Chapter 13

The next morning, Iris was sitting on a wall in the corner of the courtyard, lost in a book, when Lady Melfort and the falconer entered the courtyard, deep in conversation. They seemed guilty and surreptitious. Iris hesitated – but they had not seen her, so she remained where she was in the shadows.

The falconer was saying, 'She makes incredible demands. She's like a blackbird that makes an offering to a mate – a present of a stone – and then expects sex.' For a mad moment, Iris thought they were talking about her. But he went on, 'She helps heal the birds, and then expects some titbit of gossip. She seems to know everything that goes on in the glen. I would rather she just made her demands.'

'It's because you feel guilty. She's had to learn the art of manipulation because she can't leave her room. And she can't leave her room because of *you*,' Lady Melfort said.

'And *you* haven't spoken to her since she took to her room. Hardly sisterly behaviour.'

'It's impossible to have a relationship with her. She's not normal. As you very well know. And ever since Daphne Tennant died she's got even worse – skulking away in the nursery, casting her imaginary spells and plotting my family's downfall.'

'Nothing's normal round here,' grumbled the falconer.

Iris was surprised by the familiar way the falconer was talking to his mistress. She wondered if he knew something about Lady Melfort's family that gave him a hold over her.

Iris remained in the shade and watched as they walked out of sight. She strolled to the centre of the courtyard where

75

they had been standing a moment earlier, and looked up. Agnes was standing at the open window, like the Lady of Shalott. '*The mirror cracked from side to side*,' Iris thought. '"*The curse has come upon me*," *cried the Lady of Shalott*.' Agnes beckoned Iris to come up.

Agnes had started feeding some seeds to the blackbird. To Iris' surprise, it was flapping its wings with apparent ease. The bird seemed to have healed uncannily quickly. The two women walked onto the balcony, and Agnes scattered the rest of the seeds onto the bird table while Iris sat down on a cane chair.

Edward was walking in the garden down below, and crossed into their line of vision.

'A good-looking man, don't you think?'

Iris looked down at him for a moment. She then turned round and saw the Lady of Shalott smiling at her, a rather sly smile, as if she had been reading Iris' thoughts and they had amused her greatly.

'There were rumours that Daphne was pregnant,' Agnes said. Agnes looked down at the ground, in *faux* bashfulness. She was a fantasist, Iris decided. She wondered if she could believe anything this woman said to her.

An arcane book lying on the balcony floor beside her chair caught her eye. It was a book of witchcraft, opened up at a spell that listed herbal ingredients: rosebay willowherb, foxglove and nasturtiums. Symbols covered the pages. The spell was titled: *On Summoning up Queen Mab, Midwife to the Faeries*. Iris struggled to her feet, feeling dizzy.

'Here, let me help you.'

She felt Agnes' claws on her arms.

She pulled away.

'It's fine. I can manage. I just feel a bit faint.'

The summer night was still, and the full moon hung in the sky as Iris took a walk across the moor. The grass and heather were turfy beneath her feet. The world was casting its spell over her as she gazed upon it, but her motive for being there ran through her, like the line of quartz crystal through granite.

Iris saw a heavy figure walking towards her, just as if it had risen up out of the rocky ground: Edward's brutish face and deep-set eyes were emphasized by the moonlight. His sullen body seemed to have been hewn out of the glen itself, metamorphosed.

This place is his, she thought, he's heir to it, but it seems to own him on this night. He has become its servant, its plaything. And what am I in relation to him, and this place? – a blade of grass, a tiny white anemone, a piece of fool's gold. At his heart lies a powerful indifference. I am the shadow that his body casts upon the ground, and in order to do what I must do, I must remain so.

They walked back together, slowly, to the entrance hall of the castle. An owl leapt up from the portal, and with ghostly wings fluttered into the trees. Edward's face was unreadable in the gloomy doorway. She was aware, as she looked up at him, of the moon shining full on her face. Its light was betraying her, she thought. Betraying who she really was, betraying her desire. She moved until she was in the shadow of his body, in vain.

'In the shadow, you remind me of someone else,' he said.

Her heart quickened.

'I have known who you are since I first saw you in the pool. You have the same voice. And you're becoming more like her every day.'

'Why didn't you tell me?'

'Why didn't *you* tell *me*?'

They smiled at each other.

'Why haven't you told your family?' she persisted.

He looked down at her. 'I wanted to find out more about you first.'

'And have you found out enough yet?' she asked. But he didn't reply. 'Edward, you will be on my side? Help me find out what happened to her?'

He smiled gently. 'Of course, Iris. But isn't it obvious?'

'Obvious?'

'Obvious that she killed herself.' He opened the door for her. 'You're shivering. You should go in.'

She was loathe to go inside, for so many reasons – but she entered the castle, and did not turn to look back on his half-smiling death-face.

Iris waited until lunchtime the next day, when the whole family were seated in the dining-room, before climbing the staircase swiftly and noiselessly. As she opened the door to the Cabinet of Curiosities, she felt the cold air of the room reach in to the back of her throat.

She walked across the chequered floor to the Glen Almain cabinet. She unlocked the drawer and took the suicide note out of its envelope. She read the three words that were written in green ink – the same green ink that Lord Melfort used on the margins of his secret files: *'I am sorry.'* But it was not the words that mattered; it was how they were written. *They were not in her sister's handwriting.* It looked foreign, tortuous, a cuckoo of a letter, the clumsy lettering disguising the true identity of the writer. She thought she would gain some insight into her sister's death, and now nothing – just pretend words.

Who had forged the note and why? The fact that it was written in green ink meant little. Anyone could have borrowed Lord Melfort's ink, or have green ink of their own. Had Louis stolen the note because he knew it wasn't genuine? To prevent further, closer examination by the police? Iris' mind was becoming confused with possibilities. She was drawing up a list of names – not of the war dead, but of the men who lived in the glen. The glen was driving her mad, as it had driven her sister mad. *Fantasizing about murder.*

She heard footsteps outside in the corridor. Quickly, she put the note back and locked the drawer. She returned the key to its proper place just before Louis walked into the room. His long hair was moving back from side to side with

78

a momentum all of its own. It had energy. That was what desire was – energy; it didn't matter whether it was positive or negative, the energy of desire.

'Iris, what a surprise to find you here. Did you find what you were looking for?'

She tried to look innocent.

He smiled at her. 'You seem to be spying on everyone, Iris. Listening at doors.' Then suddenly he snarled at her, 'Stop nosing around my room!'

'Why? Because Daphne Tennant's suicide note is hidden in one of your cabinets?'

Louis turned pale. 'She was important to me.'

'So you just stole it. The police might have found it rather interesting, don't you think? '

Louis didn't reply.

'I thought you said that everything in your Cabinet of Curiosities was authentic? You do realize the note is a fake, don't you? Is that the real reason you took it – to stop the police from examining it? Do you know who wrote it?'

'I can't tell you.'

'You mean you won't.'

'You're only interested because you're Daphne's sister.' He spat out the words.

'How long have you known?'

'Edward has just told me.'

Iris felt a sharp pang of betrayal – she had never known such an intense feeling before.

'And because you think the note is fake, you suspect she may have been murdered!' He sounded contemptuous. 'But mightn't it be *you* who's responsible for your sister's death?'

'What are you talking about?'

'Daphne would often talk about how you never loved her as a sister should.'

'I don't believe you.'

'She and I were very intimate.'

Of course, she thought, Daphne would have slept with

Louis. She could rarely resist her passionate nature. Louis would have intrigued her, as he had, to her surprise, intrigued Iris too. His dark eyes in their hollowed-out face had transformed into the eyes of a magpie.

'She told me how jealous you were of her.'

She turned her back on him so that he could not see her twisted face. Then she turned back.

'So you think, somehow, *I could have stopped her killing herself*?'

'Isn't that really what *you're* saying? Unconsciously. You think that someone besides Daphne herself is responsible for her death. And you're right. What you can't accept is that the person responsible is *you*.'

She slapped him across the face. Her hand stung with the pain. He only flinched momentarily, as a red weal spread across his face.

'Don't ever say that again,' she cried. 'Say that I am responsible for her death. I was nowhere near. I was nowhere near!'

'But you are now. You are close, aren't you? Close to her.'

She felt like crying. She had to stop those tears coming, stop them pouring down her face. How she hated those possible tears. They would be a betrayal, every one of them: a betrayal of her own potent confusion.

People, deep down, know when others need help. In dreams they have an aura of vulnerability. The air is shivery around them, like a mirage. Their faces indistinct like the faces of the supernatural. Daphne had needed her; she should somehow have known. She had simply not wanted to know.

The rain poured down outside the window as if the whole world were crying tears. It was late – a coldness had descended on her room at the castle, and she bent down to put some more logs on the fire. The flames leapt up, flickering alive with their own enigmatic power.

80

Iris had been an observer all her life. She had entered the glen as an observer, but was gradually becoming involved in the story of her sister's death. Her questioning had begun as a need for a cold rational understanding of why Daphne had died, but transformed into an emotional net from which she was struggling to break free. It was a net that she had flown into with her eyes wide open. The holes had been so big and wide that she had not noticed the strings that delineated them until they were digging into her skin.

But she couldn't see whose hand was pulling the net tighter around her – sometimes she felt it was her own. And that this was what she had to do, to understand her sister's death fully. That the only way to find out the truth was to become emotionally implicated, to feel as her sister had felt, to do what her sister had done, to become a kind of sacrifice.

Chapter 14

Iris woke up in the middle of the night and couldn't get back to sleep. The moon was shining through her window. She went to the window and looked out; Edward was walking down one of the garden paths. She flung on some clothes and followed him out. A bat skimmed her head, its wings fluttering. Edward had disappeared, but the heads of the statues peered over the hedges at her.

Iris walked behind the circular hedge that hid the statue of Daphne. Moonlight had transformed the stone to marble. Approaching it, Iris noticed another inscription carved into its plinth on the other side:

> *Help me, Peneus! Open the earth to enclose me,*
> *or change my form, which has brought me into*
> *this danger!*

Strand by strand, Iris started to pull the ivy off the statue's face. At first, the plant clung tightly to the stone, its lecherous tentacles loathe to let go. She tore away the ivy's corpse-like fingers to reveal the fine features of her own sister's face.

Edward had sculpted her and Iris could tell, from the intimate lines and curves of her voluptuous body, that Edward had known Daphne's body too. The eyes of the statue looked out at her creator with longing and petrified desire.

She felt a hand on her shoulder; she turned to see Edward standing beside her.

'I came to join you,' she said. 'I saw you from my window.'

'It was terrible, what happened to Daphne. Terrible. '

His eyes were downcast, his face had grown white. She felt as if she had become pinned to the ground.

'She was precious to me.' His voice had become almost inaudible. 'You've no idea how precious.'

She tried to gauge the feeling in his voice, to quantify it. It was a hidden pain that had come up from the past and replaced present reality. It wiped the present clean and threatened who he was.

'She was very sensual. She had utter belief in herself,' he said quietly.

'But not at the end. '

'No. Not at the end.'

With a sudden drowning wave of realization, Iris understood the depth of Edward's relationship with her sister. 'It was *you* who put her in that luxurious room, bought her expensive clothes – Daphne was your *mistress*.'

The words seemed to choke in her throat. She had always been jealous of her younger sister, of her sensuality and her ability to feel and experience life in a way that Iris could only dream about. And now it was Daphne whom Edward had desired, whom he *still* desired. Not her.

The shadows of the clouds moved swiftly over the mountains and fields, like the wings of dark birds. One moment a field turned yellow-gold in the light; the next it was plunged into gloom. The paper-thin pale blue harebells wavered in the wind.

As Iris walked through the glen the trees creaked, their leafy branches scraping the sky in circular movements. A kestrel in the sky hovered still against the wind, then took a dip upwards and away, surrendering – half-flying, half-carried – to the current.

She found the falconer flying his bird at the top of the moor.

'You know why Daphne died, don't you?' she asked him.

He didn't answer her directly, but said instead, 'I'm not supposed to be on the moor with my falcon. The gamekeeper is frightened for his precious grouse. Do you know, the parents of my bird are pinned to his front door? But she's sharp set. And so am I.'

His eyes looked like his birds', all of a sudden not human, but empty and full of will.

'You should leave the glen. It will be dangerous for you to stay.'

'Is that a threat?'

'What do you take me for? I'm not threatening you. I'm just warning you.'

The falcon was flying towards them. He put out his arm and the bird landed on it, its wings outstretched. The peregrine then quickly shut up its wings, folded them in like a mechanical puppet. Iris waited for the falcon to settle.

'What do you mean?' she asked. 'Is it to do with Daphne? Or my work for Lord Melfort?'

'Iris,' he said. 'It's too dangerous for me to tell you anything. You wouldn't understand, anyway. And even without telling you, it's dangerous for you to stay.' The falcon started to pick fiercely at the meat in his outstretched hand.

The falconer knew something about her sister's death, certainly. His still manner concealed a steel knowledge about primitive drives. Things done without thinking, on instinct. He worked with birds of prey; of course he knew about violence, about the art of death.

Chapter 15

As Iris walked back to the castle, she saw Agnes signalling from her window. She entered her room, and saw that Agnes' usually fluid body had crystallized with anger.

'So you've been with the falconer again. I expect he's tried to make you leave the glen. Ignore him, Iris. He's threatened me too. He sees me as a wild bird that needs to be controlled. He told me that owls were the most vicious birds of prey of all.'

Iris looked at her large owl-eyes and silver hair, astounded. How, she wondered, did anyone think they could tame her? The only thing Agnes seemed able to love was her birds, and she flooded them with all the tenderness she could not feel for others or for herself. Iris caught sight of the encrusted bird table, and she remembered the bird Agnes said she was waiting for: the bird of paradise who never came to her table.

Agnes was saying coldly, 'My family want you to stay.'

'So they all know why I'm here?'

'Oh, I expect so, by now.'

'But why don't they want me to leave? I'm here under false pretences. I'm asking awkward questions.'

'They think you'll be useful.'

This woman, Iris realized, was wielding power over her: the power of knowledge. Trapped in her room, Agnes had little conventional sway – so instead, she took and exchanged information. She beguiled and bartered.

Agnes looked out of the window and said quietly, for effect, 'There's something I think you should know. From my doorway, I saw someone go into your sister's bedroom,

85

after she had gone missing. They were carrying a letter.'

'You mean the fake suicide note?'

Agnes gave her an enigmatic smile. Agnes' opaqueness, her circumlocutions, were part of her trickery, Iris thought. She was only a charlatan.

'Did you see what he looked like?'

'Who said it was a man? The person was in the shadows. It could have been a man. He had the stature of an older man.'

'You mean Lord Melfort? He couldn't have had anything to do with Daphne's death. It's quite impossible. He thinks of nothing but his work. You're playing games with me, Agnes. Trying to cause trouble for the family.'

Iris was taken aback by how hurt and angry she felt on Lord Melfort's behalf; how much like a father to her he had become.

The next morning, Iris walked into the castle's entrance hall from the garden. Her way was blocked by Lady Melfort. She looked furious.

'So you came here to spy on us. Daphne's sister. I should have guessed. You seem so uptight, but really underneath it all you're just like her. A common little slut.'

Margaret Melfort turned her back on Iris and walked slowly down the corridor that was so heavily festooned with the dusty flags of her ancestry.

'Who are *you* really?' Iris asked, her words echoing down the corridor after Lady Melfort. 'You expect such different treatment, don't you, Lady Melfort? Because of who you are. Your whole life is based on concern for your public persona. Your servants, buildings, gardens – they are what make up who you are. But who are *you*, really?'

Lady Melfort whirled round. 'You do know, don't you Iris, that the mother cuckoo chooses a nest containing birds' eggs that are the same colour as her own? The cuckoo throws one egg out, and replaces it with her own egg. The natural mother then rears the cuckoo chick as her own, and the cuckoo chick, as it grows bigger, gradually throws the rest of the eggs out of the nest.

'Aren't you, Iris, that cuckoo chick in the nest? You seem to be the same colour as us. You have lived in our house and eaten our food. We have welcomed you into the glen, made you one of us – but you have other reasons for being here.'

She walked up the castle staircase, and Iris followed her. On the landing, Lady Melfort took a deep breath. Saliva was foaming at her mouth like *cuckoo spit*. Her thin, wet lips were trembling but otherwise her face was very still. Her eyes were dry, and hard as lapis lazuli.

'A cuckoo. That's what you are. Living off us, in order to get what you want – to find out what you need, in order to survive. You think that by finding out why your sister died, you will make your small, drab life worth living. And you don't care if, in the process, you destroy us all.'

Iris looked at her. She didn't know what to say. It was typical of Lady Melfort to see so unequivocally into the black hearts of others; Lady Melfort was not naïve. She looked for the worst in people, and was triumphant when she found it. And it was true that Iris had found a nest and made it her own.

But Iris felt that she had justice on her side. That was something that Lady Melfort, with her aristocratic hubris, would always refuse to see. She would see the affront to her great family, but never the pain that they themselves had caused. They always acted with impunity, whatever they did was above reproach, but God protect anyone who did them any harm.

'How right you are. How painfully right. I'm here to find out the truth. And I'm not sorry if the truth disturbs you, or destroys your family. I'm not sorry at all.'

In a sudden frenzied impulse, Lady Melfort lunged at her. In spite of being so thin, Lady Melfort had her own manic energy, her own hidden strength.

Iris instinctively stepped aside and Lady Melfort tumbled down the staircase, as if in slow motion, as if she were

87

falling slowly through water. She seemed unharmed until she reached the step at the bottom, where her body landed awkwardly. Iris heard the cracking of bones. Lady Melfort lay on the ground, her limbs askew like a broken puppet. Her eyes remained open, staring up at the domed ceiling as if reluctant to lose sight of her beloved castle.

A few of the servants came running out into the hall. Iris was still standing on the landing.

'She fell,' she said, quietly. 'She slipped and fell. You'd better call the doctor.'

The butler knelt down at Lady Melfort's side and took up her hand gently, feeling for her pulse. There was no expression on his face. Had he been waiting for her to die? Is that what servants did, under the guise of obsequious service and loyal devotion – wait for their masters and mistresses to die?

'Lord Melfort is in Berlin. At the Olympic Games, with visiting MPs and dignitaries. Try and inform him immediately,' Iris ordered him. 'Where is Edward?'

'On the loch, sailing, Miss Drummond,' the butler replied, giving her an enigmatic look.

She ran down the avenue to the loch, where the boat was becalmed, and shouted over to him, 'Your mother has had an accident!' Edward immediately let down the main sail and pulled out the oars from under the seat. With a set face, he started rowing vigorously to shore, the oars splashing loudly in the calm water. As he reached the shallows he leapt out into the water and pulled the boat to shore.

'What happened?' Edward asked, as they started walking quickly towards the castle.

For an instinctive moment, Iris wanted to hold him – but she recollected herself. 'Your mother fell down the stairs. We were having an argument. It was an accident,' she repeated.

Iris looked for emotion on Edward's face, but he remained impassive. His eyes had grown dull.

On arriving at the castle, they discovered that Lady Melfort had lost consciousness. They waited for the ambulance to arrive.

'You had better come with me,' Edward said to Iris. 'You saw what happened.' She could feel his hidden anger.

Edward drove without speaking, following the ambulance's tortuous route along the glen and on to the local hospital, several miles away.

After they had waited an hour in the waiting room, a solemn young doctor escorted them to Lady Melfort. They walked past beds that were filled with long-term wounded soldiers and on to Lady Melfort's private ward. There she was, lying unconscious still, her ribs swathed in bandages.

A nurse came up to the doctor and said, 'We've had to give her a large amount of morphine.'

Iris could not say anything; her mind had shut down. She looked round at Edward. His face as always was self-contained. Iris sat down beside the bed.

'Lady Melfort,' she whispered.

But it was like talking to a statue or to someone dead.

She did not know whether Lady Melfort would die. She seemed nearer to death than life. On the other hand, Daphne had always seemed very far from death.

Edward gently took Iris's hand. 'We mustn't stay too long. We're doing no good here. She will pull through. She is strong. She's not going to let go of life lightly.'

Iris pulled her hand away and fell down on her knees by the bed. 'Don't die.' she murmured. 'Don't die.'

The doctor and nurse looked embarrassed at this display of emotion. Edward firmly pulled her to the feet.

'*You're not doing any good*,' he said, sternly.

'Leave me a moment alone with her. Please.' And before Edward could reply, the doctor led him away in conversation.

Lady Melfort lay on the bed, the oxygen cylinder pumping rhythmically beside her. Her eyes were closed and Iris could make out the fine veins on her paper thin eyelids. The veined threads on her forehead stood out in lurid purple. Her mouth was shut in a straight line, as if it had said all it could ever want to say. Iris sat down on the bed beside her and took her claw-like hand.

'I didn't mean for you to fall.'

She clutched the woman's hand harder, felt the long, thin bones of her fingers, willed her to regain consciousness. Margaret Melfort gave a long sigh and opened her eyes. They seemed unseeing. She began whispering, like the wind through the trees, but Iris couldn't understand the words. She bent over her, putting her ear close to her lips.

'*You mustn't betray us*,' Margaret was saying, over and over again. '*You mustn't betray us*.'

Chapter 16

Iris was becoming irrationally possessed by a desire to bring Daphne back from the dead: to cross over to the other side and bring her back. This force of feeling was manifest throughout the glen, in all its shapes and forms. She was determined to lead Daphne back over to the living world. Not only for Daphne's sake, but to alleviate the guilt that she was starting to feel for not having loved her enough. This guilt had begun to grow like a heavy stone inside her, a rock-child that she was bearing.

A few days after Lady Melfort's fall, Iris returned to the pool and gazed down into the water. Daphne, her crocus-coloured hair floating around her, looked back up at her with beautiful, mocking eyes. Iris plunged her hand into the pool to pull her out – and felt her sister's hard strong hand grab her own. But Daphne began to pull her down into the pool and Iris felt herself teetering on the edge of the water. Summoning all her strength, Iris pulled even harder, until finally she dragged Daphne out of the pool with a last violent tug. Her naked wet sister stood on the bank, tears running down her face.

'Don't cry,' Iris said. 'There's no need to cry any more – see, I've brought you back to this side of life.'

'But I'm sick. Very sick,' Daphne replied.

Little blisters were starting to pin-prick her skin. The pale gold pustules looked harmless, but Iris was disconcerted by the way they patterned over her body so specifically.

'What are they?' Iris asked.

She could see fear in Daphne's eyes at the unconscionable power of disease.

'They won't go away. They are the sickness of the glen.'

Iris watched as the blisters turned to black weals spreading all over her sister's body. Daphne began to cough – a terrible hacking cough. Before Iris could stop her Daphne had turned and dived back into the pool, where her body vanished into the dark water. Iris was devastated at seeing her sister so ill. She felt as if her own flesh might peel away with uncertainty and fear.

'Will you help me plant this magnolia?' Hector asked Iris in the garden, that afternoon. 'Some wild animal pulled it up.' A strong scent of lavender and earth, a mixture of sweetness and soily goodness, was emanating from the ground.

She brought over the peat and watched while he re-dug the hole with his heavy spade. It must have been a large animal, thought Iris, to have pulled up such a tree. The hole it had left behind was immense – mounds of earth were scattered all around. The ground had spewed up red soil, and she helped Hector to mix it up with the peat.

Hector lowered the magnolia tree back into the hole, its huge white lantern flowers with crimson splashes trembling delicately like bells. Together they knelt at its roots and filled in the hole with their hands. Then, both still kneeling, Hector took her hands in his own and brushed the soil from them. After he had finished, he let them fall to her side.

'How is Lady Melfort?' he asked.

'She's making a good recovery.'

'She hasn't remembered how she fell?'

Iris shook her head as they both rose to their feet.

Hector nodded. 'She's forgotten about me too. A good thing, I think. Sometimes, when two people who are very close do something together against their nature, it tears them apart.'

'You mean you and Lady Melfort? I saw you kissing.'

'No. I mean she and her husband. She turned to me for consolation.'

'Consolation?'

'Lord and Lady Melfort take their role as guardians of their estate very seriously.'

'And they failed to protect Daphne.'

'You could put it like that.'

'But I keep seeing Daphne in the glen. Am I going mad?'

'When the police followed Coll to Daphne's body, hawks had already begun pecking at her eyes.'

Controlling herself, she asked, 'Why are you telling me this?'

'To make you understand that Daphne is dead. There are no ghosts. There's a fine line between insanity and fantasy. It's just your imagination.'

Hector then retreated into the glen's conspiracy of silence, like a snail into his shell.

In August a round of house parties and shooting began, which Iris and the servants dutifully watched from the sidelines. Lady Melfort was now rarely seen in public. Since the accident, her hold on the household had weakened due to an increasing reclusiveness.

One day, just before lunchtime, Iris heard a car draw up into the courtyard. She looked out of her bedroom window. The car was a black Daimler with diplomatic numberplates; it also carried the insignia of the German diplomatic corps. She watched as a man climbed out, a trilby obscuring his face, and just for a moment he looked up at her window. The reflection of the sun refracting off the glass meant that he could not see her. It was the same man who had entered her train carriage on her journey up to the glen.

Iris ran down the stairs to join him in the courtyard. Heinrich Berger smiled as she approached him.

'Why, Miss Tennant, we meet again.'

She noticed that he used her real name.

'I thought you reminded me of someone!' he exclaimed. 'It was Daphne, of course.'

He waited while the servants took his suitcases. 'Are you enjoying your work in the glen? It is a lovely place.

Unfortunately, I am just here for a few days.'

Iris nodded. He was showing her such elaborate courtesy; she wondered why she was feeling so uncomfortable in his presence.

'You'll probably never want to leave. Nature is a powerful force. In Germany we have huge respect for it. Even idolize it. But I imagine that is a very unBritish thing to do!'

'I suppose that here, we tend to think *we* have dominion over *it*.'

'And really it is the other way round, is it not? And the sooner your nation understands the power of instinct, the sooner you will reach true greatness. Reason is greatly overestimated. We are all part of nature. Man is a natural warrior. If we forget this, we become weak.'

Iris simply looked at him.

'And you, Miss Tennant. Perhaps you are not as reasonable as you once were. Perhaps Glen Almain is changing you. Is that not true?'

'I do feel different. But I hope not to lose reason altogether.'

Later that afternoon, working in the library, she became distracted by the shots of the grouse shooters on the moor. The Melforts' life of leisure was a mixture of nature and high society, the sensual and the social.

The shooters would return to the castle exhausted and triumphant, death and blood on their hands. By killing they had distracted Death from themselves, for a moment. She wondered if her sister's death had made someone's life seem less mortal.

The noise of the shooting continued to disturb her, and she decided to take a walk along the edge of the loch. It was a heady summer's day with the grass pollen dense in the air and the bees humming. Her thoughts seemed to swim like fish just below the surface of a pool.

She stopped on the shore to look out over the loch. She could see two men moving about on the isle. She withdrew into the shadows of an oak and watched as Lord Melfort and Heinrich Berger began walking along the edge of the island, deep in conversation. Lord Melfort's words carried clearly over the water to where she stood.

'Don't worry, Heinrich. I have the Gruinard files. It's now just a question of trust. You must be patient.'

Just then a shot rang out on the moor, causing both men to look round. Iris swiftly withdrew further into the shade of the tree. A grouse from the moor flew up into the air and then fell heavily from the sky. Iris felt the blood of the chase, but she also fell with the bird. She waited for the men to cross to the other side of the isle, before coming out into the sunlight.

She encountered Edward in the castle courtyard, carrying a brace of grouse.

'My parents are holding a party in a few weeks time,' he said. 'Would you do me the honour of accompanying me?'

His face was flushed with the excitement of the kill.

Iris nodded her acceptance.

However, that night, she woke up in a state of panic in a darkened room. She could hardly breathe. I want to leave, she thought; I have to leave the glen, otherwise I will risk losing my mind.

Early next morning she packed her suitcase. She would start walking to the station a few miles away. Perhaps a car might pass and give her a lift. The sun was shining when she started off, but by the time she had reached the end of the glen road, it was raining heavily. No car had come and she was becoming soaked.

The glen had drawn Daphne to it, pulled Daphne towards it with its siren call. It had held her in its thrall. And now, as Iris walked along the roman road to the station, the glen was pulling Iris back. She could hear its distant voice like the undulating note of the curlew, smell the heavy scent of the densely-packed fern and the acrid odour of the gorse leaves.

Chapter 17

When she arrived back at the castle, no-one had noticed she had left; the family were all still at breakfast. She climbed the stairs to Agnes' room and was about to knock on her door when she heard raised voices coming from inside.

'Don't you understand what you're doing?' the falconer was shouting. 'If Iris finds out the truth, she will betray us all.'

'Perhaps. It's no more than we deserve.'

Iris, as she peered through the narrow gap in the door, was struck by the naked *emotion* on Agnes' face, the anger and pain. She was no longer a sly enchantress but a mortal woman. Iris saw the way she looked at the falconer. In spite of Agnes' apparent antagonism towards him she was giving him the look of love. The most dangerous emotion in the glen is love, not hate, Iris thought. It is the falconer who is really her rare bird, her bird of paradise.

'It's been ten years!' the falconer shouted at her.

Ten years since his rejection of her. They had not even kissed. But his rejection had been so cruel. Agnes had joined him on a walk across the moor. For the first time, she had reached out for his hand. She could feel the blood pulse in his palm. He had pulled away so decisively, then turned to meet her gaze with no compunction.

'You are too old,' he said.

And she saw, reflected in his eyes, a childless woman with parched skin. She saw herself as he saw her, and all her phantom versions of herself fell away and she was left only with this aged shroud.

96

She took to her room. And after a while she found she could not leave. She could reach the door, place her hand on the brass-cold handle, but she could not turn it. She would try, the sweat pouring from her forehead as the birdsong outside her window grew too loud. What had started off as a gesture of pain became her way of life.

She would watch him from the window as he flew his falcon and fantasize about flying free, about holding his absolute attention the way his falcon did. However, he would never turn to look at her although she was sure he must be aware of her, so strong was the intensity of her gaze. But no, he never turned. She watched the falcon in the air, having spotted her prey, her wings fluttering up and down rapidly, her head and tail down, her body arched like a bow.

Agnes' mouth tasted bitter. And she knew then she would never love again. And she also knew she would not let another love him. Or him love another. As her life had petrified, so would his.

'Leave Iris alone!' pleaded the falconer. 'Stop helping her. I'm frightened for the glen.'

'You mean you're frightened for yourself. What you're *really* worried about is Iris helping *me*! You're scared of what *I* can do to *you*. You're frightened of my witchcraft.'

Agnes turned, and caught sight of Iris spying on them through the door. The original mask-like expression returned, clamped to her face. She had regained her power.

'Why don't you come in, Iris? You must be uncomfortable out there, standing in that awkward position.'

The falconer barged past Agnes and Iris and out of the room, his footsteps fading away down the corridor.

'He's no idea of the suffering he has caused me. Or if he does, he doesn't care. I'll change him into the only creature he has truly loved. Fetch his gauntlet for me, Iris, and I will answer any question you want.'

'So you *are* a witch!'

'What's going on in Germany seems to me more like the

witchcraft madness of the Middle Ages. Hitler speaks of the "magic power of the spoken word." And there is Xavier, and our scientists, all making up their own evil potions. Their own cauldron of germs. Men have their own witchcraft.'

Iris felt overawed and frightened. For the powers in this room seemed now to take on a life of their own; complicated, jagged, like the jaws of a trap. She had to find a way of getting out of the room but she felt inexplicably unable to move, as if she had become rooted to the ground while Agnes, standing at the window, just stared at her.

A few days later, Iris took a walk amongst the last dry remains of August. The air was full of the honey scent of the heather covered hills. Louis suddenly appeared in front of her as if out of nowhere, his expression volatile. By his side stood Muriel. Her face looked twisted. It was as if vines were growing over her, Iris thought, entwining her in their leafy grasp. She looked like a nymph turning into a tree, her thoughts growing convoluted as the twisting vine.

'I hear Edward is taking you to the dance,' Louis said, accusingly.

She nodded. Muriel was now looking embarrassed.

'You should be careful of him.'

'What do you mean?'

'Shouldn't we go, Louis?' Muriel said, tugging at his sleeve.

'Leave me alone!' he shouted at his sister.

'I hate this family!' Muriel shouted back, bursting into tears and running off back down the hill.

He turned round to Iris again. 'Do you know why Edward came back a war hero, Iris? Because he found it easy to kill. He's a man only of his senses, of his own pleasure. Perhaps Daphne didn't give him what he wanted.'

'You're now accusing *him* of murder? I thought *I* was supposed to be responsible for her suicide?'

'Perhaps I was wrong.'

She looked at Louis. His face always seemed to be on the

edge of some emotion: anger, tears or laughter. But this time his fine features, generally so mobile, had become petrified by the coldness of his words. She felt uncertain, as if the ground was falling away from beneath her feet.

Anyone in Glen Almain, she thought, could have murdered Daphne. Could not even she murder in a moment of madness, a moment of passion? She imagined emotions taking hold of her and ransacking her body; holding her reason hostage to let primitive feelings take over her.

'I wonder, Iris, if you believe in what you're doing any more. Do you really think you're going to find out what happened to her?' Louis asked.

'Of course. That's why I'm still here.'

'No, you're still here because you're falling in love with Edward. Don't you see, he's using you? That's why he didn't tell us who you were before. So he could lead you on more easily.'

'But why?'

'My father might need your help.'

Anger welled up in Iris. 'You're just jealous of my friendship with him, Louis.'

But he ignored this.

'And it's worked, Iris. It's too late for you to leave the glen, now. Can't you see that? Because of Edward.'

Chapter 18

Iris crept along the corridor of the East Wing and opened the door to Daphne's room. Late afternoon light poured onto the crystal chandelier, almost blinding her with its iridescent glass. She opened the mirrored wardrobe and began to search through the dresses hanging there until she found a leaf-green chiffon gown, a dress that Queen Mab might have worn. She returned to her room. The light was just darkening, but the traces of a hot afternoon hung at the open window.

Later that evening, Iris walked out into the balmy night. The chiffon of the dress brushed against her skin, as insubstantial as the evening air. As she walked toward the garden, the hem trailing in the grass, her hair gradually uncurled itself from her chignon to fall in tendrils around her face. Iris felt herself to be disappearing into the sensation of the night sky and stars, a deep flickering of light and dark.

The silver beeches were beckoning down from their heights, their luminous bark like water. The trees that arched down the avenue seemed to be leading her away from the castle, their branches spiking out into the dusk.

As Iris approached the garden, she could hear the strains of jazz weaving its way through the air, the melodic rhythmic music mingling with the sound of dancing and laughter. This place is now full of desire, she thought.

Desire. That word resounded in her head every time she took a step, the heel of her shoes clicking on the path like the ticking of a clock. The garden and marquee were already full of guests for the dance. Sheathed in sparkling fabrics, undulating women stood bewitching the night air.

Iris entered the throng. She could become one of those guests, she thought; shed her skin of outsider, servant, *voyeur*. She would blend into this rapturous occasion, laugh and drink champagne.

Moving through the party, she searched in vain for a familiar face. She was looking for Edward but could see no-one she knew. The women appeared vivacious but blankly beautiful and looked away when she caught their eyes. Hawk-like or cherubic men stared down at her with imperious indifference. She was not meant to be here, after all. She did not belong. She turned to walk back through the crowd again, to leave, to escape, and she had just reached the entrance of the courtyard, seen the avenue of trees waiting for her, when her arm was gently seized.

She whirled round and saw Edward.

'Where do you think you're going?' He looked different, flushed, as if the vivacity of the party had infected him.

'I shouldn't be here.'

'What do you mean?'

She nodded to the crowd of partygoers, laughing and talking and dancing in the moonlight. Edward took a loose strand of her hair, and deliberately tucked it behind her ear. His eyes did not seem to register that she was wearing Daphne's dress.

'They party because they're hanging onto dear life. They've just come in disguise. You, little cuckoo, do not have the monopoly on pain.'

Their eyes met for a moment; she was taken aback by the look he gave her. It was full of intense need – not how she had thought him. He took her hand and led her back into the centre of the crowd and they began to dance. It was a third person, this dance they were performing. No, more than a person, a laughing god that lived in their steps and their moving bodies. A laughing Bacchanalian god was dissolving the material world around them.

'But Iris, you've come in disguise too. You've come dressed as your sister,' he shouted over the music. He offered her his

101

arm. 'Come, walk with me in the garden.'

Candles decorated the gardens and in the moonlight each leaf or rose petal was clearly delineated, as if outlined by ink. As they walked, the clamour and the noise of the party fell away. Like nocturnal butterflies, bats danced above their heads then vanished into the night.

Edward led Iris under the black canopy of the yew tree. The ancient tree was centuries old, the ground thick with yew needles, the earth dry as dust. Here it had been completely sheltered from sunlight and rain. The tree spread like an awning high over their heads, its heavy branches sweeping down to the ground. Edward and Iris were encaged in darkness, except for the slivers of moonlight shining through the leaves.

Iris felt an odd kind of happiness, as if she couldn't quite contain who she was. The hooting of an owl sounded out ominous and primitive. She looked at Edward's profile in the yew's darkness. His silhouette was strange and distant. He looked like a bull, she thought; a minotaur. A minotaur trapped in a labyrinth.

He appeared, she realized with a surge of compassion, alone. Is that what she wanted from him, his solitude? She felt his arm encircle her waist as he brought her towards him. As he bent his head down to kiss her, he extinguished the remaining light. The darkness highlighted the touch of his lips.

They came out from the canopy of the tree and sat down together on some stone steps. Edward took out a cigarette case and lighter from his pocket. He struck the flint and lit a cigarette. The potent scent of his cigarette smoke mingled with the fresh air.

'You're so quiet sometimes, Iris, I never know what you're thinking.'

'I never know what *you're* thinking.'

'Yes, you do.'

Before she had time to respond, he pulled at Daphne's dress and ripped it off her shoulder in gossamer shreds, revealing her breasts and her shoulders which gleamed whitely in the moonlight.

Is this what he had done to Daphne? Was what had happened to her sister now happening to her?

She instinctively brought up her arms to cover herself. Edward saw the look of anger and despair in her eyes, and returned to himself.

'I'm sorry,' he said. 'You shouldn't have worn that dress.'

He took off his jacket and it shrouded her like the great dark wing of a bird.

'Let Daphne rest in peace,' he said, quietly. And now Iris no longer knew what to think or feel.

Chapter 19

The next morning, Iris looked out of her window to see the staff clearing the tables and the detritus from the garden party the evening before. Workers were slowly dismantling the marquee. Soon the gardens would be empty of all signs of the guests, all traces of what had happened there. She had already forgiven Edward for what had happened the previous evening. She blamed herself for wearing Daphne's dress. It had been an irrational, irresponsible act that had played unfairly with Edward's feelings.

Iris watched Hector walk down the garden in the direction of the greenhouse, and decided to follow him. She slipped downstairs into the garden. She stopped outside the greenhouse and gazed at him through the glass. Hector was planting geraniums in separate pots, carefully shaking their roots and dusting pollen from their crimson and yellow petals. He prodded the soil down into the pots with his stubby fingers, falling into a trance as if the earth was pulling him into itself. He had become a slave to the earth, doing what it needed and demanded of him.

He brought out the watering can and began to water the flowers. The water sprinkled down over the pots, changing the earth from grey to bluey-black, until huge globes of tears were filling the soft velvety blooms. As he watered the flowers, Iris reflected that he was made for the love of both men and women. He had a natural beauty that drew people towards him.

She was about to call out to him, when Hector suddenly strode to the end of the greenhouse with a purposefulness that aroused her curiosity. Iris circled round the outside of the greenhouse and watched as Hector opened a door to a larder at the back of the greenhouse. From where she was standing, she could see that the interior was filled with hanging game. Hector proceeded to stuff the meat into a hessian sack, and hauled the sack over his shoulders as if it was full of wood or peat. He nonchalantly carried the meat through the languishing gardens, gardens spread out in front of him as if for his own pleasure. He passed the staff who were clearing away the tables and chairs from the dance.

Iris followed him down the avenue into the glen and over the iron bridge. She followed him into the petrified forest. He stopped at the centre of the forest, where the remains of Cassie had been found. Hector emptied the bag of meat at the foot of a fossilized tree, bloody game tumbling out over the stony roots. It was where he must have led Cassie, Iris thought, unchaining her from outside the schoolhouse and bringing her here.

Hector could sense that somewhere in the forest the beast had already smelt his offering in the air: the deep, sickly smell of blood.

Later that day, Iris spied from her window Hector pruning the yew hedges. She came out into the garden, and cautiously approached him. Standing beside him, she said quietly,

'Living in the glen, you would have heard my sister's screams.'

Hector, without looking up from his work, replied, 'My only duty is to the beast.'

Iris looked at him, anew. Hector was caught up in his own laws of nature – his indifference to man wasn't a sign of strength, but a rejection of humanity. His passion for nature, his preoccupation with a mythical beast was a rejection of what made us human.

'It's my duty to protect him,' Hector said.

Chapter 20

The next morning, Iris took a stroll with Edward in the garden. The oak leaves had turned to orange and pale gold and red. They walked behind the hedge that encircled the statue of Daphne, with her petrified face looking down at them impassively. Edward's face loomed over Iris, laughing, and she responded to his kiss before she knew what she was doing. There was no hesitation, no second of doubt. He pulled back slowly.

'What about your mother?' she said, half-teasingly. 'She doesn't approve of me.'

'I don't care what she thinks, any more.'

Just then, they heard footsteps on the gravel path, and they turned to see Louis entering the enclave.

'Edward, why do you take everything I love away from me?' Louis demanded. Louis looked as he did when he battered the snake's skull into the ground, Iris thought: possessed by an evil spirit.

She imagined Louis catching sight of Daphne with Edward, over a year ago, and being subsumed by jealousy. Edward was now the inheritor, and he had taken Daphne from him too. Might Louis, on the night of Daphne's death, have followed her to the petrified forest? Ambushed her, all bird instinct, pulling at her clothes, their bodies a murderous entanglement of desire? And Daphne would not, initially, have fought back. She would have been taken by surprise, not prepared for this violent act. She would not have begun to understand what was happening.

However, Louis was now hurling himself not at her but at Edward, and as he flew through the air it was as if for a moment he had turned into a black bird. Iris screamed. Edward staggered backwards and collapsed into the statue of Daphne. The statue fell to the ground and shattered into pieces. The brothers wrestled together amongst the broken debris, until Edward finally managed to pin Louis' arms behind his back.

'Louis, everything came to me of its own accord,' Edward said. As he continued to grapple with Louis on the ground, Lady Melfort appeared round the corner of the hedge. Her sons immediately fell apart.

Edward and Louis stood up, brushing grass and dirt from their clothes. Louis looked down at the ground, but Lady Melfort and Edward just stared at each other. How upright and strong he is, Iris thought. Like an eagle. And, since her accident, Lady Melfort had grown weaker. He was no longer susceptible to her power. Now, his impenetrability protected him from her gaze like a shield. She could no longer turn him to stone.

Chapter 21

The November mountains looked like a metallic tableau of echoing tones. The silver of the bare trees imitated the silver of the sky, the bronze of the leaves, the ferns. The quick and urgent river, with its white foam encircling the rocks, reflected the smattering of snow on the mountain tops. White frost petrified the grass. Only the dense blotches of the evergreen pines looked velvet against the background of the sandy hills.

That week, Lord Melfort left for London again, and Iris watched from upstairs as his Bentley drove down the avenue under the opulent beeches. She could see his mysterious silhouette inside, his body attired in his elegant, dark London suit, so different from his thickset country tweeds

She was beginning to feel that he was the most remote, absent figure of the glen. He moved in and out of it, like Alice through the Looking Glass. She wondered which of his worlds was the real one and which world was reflected back to front – the one in the glen, or the one in London?

Even though he must have known who she was by now, still he had not mentioned Daphne to her. It was as if Daphne had never existed, never worked for him. Nor did he seem to have any relationship with his children. They were equidistant to him. They had no effect on him for good or ill. They were nothing to do with him and they, in turn, treated him with polite indifference.

Soon after he had left, Lady Melfort summoned Iris to her bedroom, where the embers in the fireplace were giving off a feverish heat. Since her fall, Lady Melfort now spent most of her day in an armchair by the fire, a cashmere blanket draped over her knees. Her attitude towards Iris over the weeks had grown softer, more benign. She seemed vulnerable – Iris realized with a shock that she herself now might be able to do anything she wanted.

'I have here the instructions my husband has left for you. I see he's still tireless in his campaign for appeasement,' Lady Melfort grumbled.

'But, Lady Melfort, even our ambassador to Berlin is pro-appeasement. He has called Hitler "The Apostle of Peace."'

'And we have let Hitler reoccupy the Rhineland! And done nothing! Must you be so naïve, Iris?'

The room was hot and claustrophobic. Iris was finding it difficult to breathe in the overheated room.

'It was your sister who used to say that Hitler was like a falconer,' Lady Melfort went on, 'using Xavier as his lure. Using my husband to attract the most powerful men in our country to his cause. She would even say it to his face. She was a very outspoken girl.'

'And what would your husband say?'

'He would laugh. Try to convince her of the error of her ways. Heinrich would even make little gifts of Nazi insignia to her. But she wasn't interested in anything to do with the National Socialists. She would hand the trinkets on to Coll – the silly boy had no idea what they meant.'

Iris carefully took the instructions from her shaking hands and left Margaret Melfort staring into the remains of the fire.

Margaret felt exhausted. After the fall, she was finding conversation increasingly tiring. She wondered if she could ever persuade Iris of her conviction that Germany was intent on war. She knew that Xavier was trying to persuade Iris otherwise.

Daphne had always seemed weak to Margaret, a victim of her susceptible temperament, but Daphne's resistance to Xavier's and Heinrich's influence had come as a surprise to her. She wondered if Iris would resist their powers of persuasion so easily.

At the time, she had felt Daphne's death to be an evil necessity. Daphne's artlessness might have caused the family trouble. There was the danger that she might even consider going to the authorities. And there had been the added scandal of the pregnancy. Lady Melfort's foremost duty had always been to the good name of her family and estate.

Margaret never openly expressed grief or guilt about what had happened to Daphne and the child. But she started to collect mourning paintings of lost children soon afterwards. And Daphne's violent death had driven her and Xavier apart. They both heard the beast calling out to them at night. Margaret Melfort suspected it was only a matter of time before her family was finally punished for the clearing of Glen Almain.

Gabbling pheasants scuttled under the bushes in the falconer's garden and perched on his gate. They were plucky, ignorant of their own lumbering as they blundered on through life. They reminded Iris of mankind – even when they flew they floundered, carrying with difficulty their plump, ponderous bodies. It was as if they were having difficulty staying up in the sky.

Iris crept up to the window and peered inside the falconer's cottage.

Muriel was standing by the mantelpiece while the falconer crouched down to stoke up his small fire and put on a saucepan of water. By the way the girl stood, gangly and precocious, Iris saw for the first time that Muriel had an energy born from the drive to get what she wanted. She had that mixture of self-interest and intelligence which verged on the sinister.

His peregrine falcon sat watching them on a wooden perch, orange flames reflected in her glistening eyes. Iris noticed the falconer's blood-stained gauntlet lying on the table. The small cottage looked cosy, and Muriel seemed

110

secure and at home there. She was a child in a woman's body, Iris thought, dangerous because she was ignorant of her own motives. Iris was sure she had the capacity to do harm, but to whom she was not sure.

As he stood up, Muriel could not stop herself: she stretched out her arm and took his hand. 'Kiss me,' Iris could hear her saying clearly through the just-open window. He turned his head away.

'Agnes is plotting against me, I can feel it. She's casting her malevolent spells,' he said.

'Why will you never kiss me? You still love Daphne, don't you? You're still obsessed by her.'

'Muriel, don't do this.'

'You're guilty, aren't you?' Muriel was almost shouting now. The falcon opened and shut its wings. 'I heard a man in the room with Daphne. Asking him to stop her going into the forest. I thought he sounded foreign, but he must have been you. You couldn't have her. So you didn't want anyone else to, either. Why wasn't I enough for you?'

'You're just a little girl compared to her.'

Tears began streaming down Muriel's face as she ran out of the room.

In December, the temperature fell dramatically. Snow covered the ground, transforming like Midas everything it touched. After a fortnight of heavy snowfalls, Iris ventured outside. She walked to the edge of the garden and saw deep paw-prints, like black hearts in the snow, leading towards the glen. Her breath pluming out into clouds, she started to follow them.

Having first welcomed the snow as cold relief, she was now starting to feel its bitterness. She continued to walk down into the glen, her determination overriding the weather. The soft white sensual snowflakes were becoming heavier and heavier, melting on her face like wet flakes of tissue paper. In spite of the cold, she continued to follow the paw-prints across the fields, trampling over the ground as if over her own will to live.

'It's a common illusion, while walking in snow, to think that you're being followed – when really it is the sound of your own footprints collapsing behind you,' Hector had once told her. She followed the paw-prints to the pool.

The pool and the waterfall had frozen over. A crow flew off from a leafless branch that overhung the iced pool. The clouds overhead possessed the luminous heavy quality of late afternoon, as if light and darkness had become one another.

She walked out onto the frozen pool. A light shift of snow fell from an overlapping branch and landed on her shoulders. As she walked on towards the waterfall a sharp crack, like a snapping of a branch, began to fissure across the pool. Iris ignored it and continued to walk across the ice until she was within touching distance of the waterfall. In the fading light, the ice of the waterfall was opaque; the water hung in suspension. Transformed by alchemy from crystal to lead.

She was standing beneath the waterfall behind which she had first kissed Louis. If it had been 'alive' it would have been gushing over her. The force of water would have been pushing her down into the pool, keeping her there, trapped beneath the surface until she drowned. But now she could reach over and touch this cold, silent inanimate matter. She looked up at the ice, tumbling down in suspension, this sepulchre of water, and saw carved into it the figure of Daphne.

Walking back up the rough path to the road, Iris noticed smoke in the distance billowing high into the sky. She thought at first it might be a bonfire, but the smoke was too dense; it was something larger, unintentional. She couldn't work out where the smoke was coming from and she began to run.

Flames were flashing up into the cold winter's day, almost invisible in the bright light. They were coming from the direction of the falconer's cottage. She ran through the snow until she reached the road. She turned a corner and, in front of her, saw that the mews had been transformed into a burning pyre.

The birds inside were flapping and calling out, and snow was dripping from the frame. Iris managed to open the door. The harris hawk was the first to fly out, its wings brushing her face as it passed by. One by one, the other birds followed the hawk up into the pale blue sky. It was then that Iris saw Muriel running down the glen through the snow towards the cliff, with the falconer in desperate pursuit.

You make me miserable, for fear you should fall and hurt yourself on these stones and I should be the cause.

By the time he reached the top of the cliff, Muriel had disappeared. The falconer looked over the drop that veered sharply down into the river below. He could see something dark at the bottom of the cliff, conspicuous against the white snow. Iris watched as he skittered down the precipitous slope, scratching and cutting himself badly on the rocks and ice. Muriel lay at the bottom, a few feet from where the river was flowing.

She was like a broken bird. Her whole body had been twisted around at a violent angle from where her neck had snapped. Her arms were outstretched like wings. As if she had leapt from the cliff like a bird, tried to fly, but instead had dropped, freewheeling on the air currents, to her death. There was no expression in her eyes, but her lips were slightly parted as if in surprise. She looked too young for death; as if death had abducted her. She lay there, looking up at the pale expanse of open sky.

He knelt down beside her. His mouth shrivelled to the little moue of a cry, like the cry of a buzzard, a mewing, keening sound. Iris saw him kiss Muriel lightly, briefly on her cold lips. He picked her up, flesh and bone weighing heavy, and flung her, unceremoniously, like a shot deer over his shoulders. He could not leave her at the bottom of the cliff for the birds or foxes.

Iris thought Muriel would not have worried about the time between leaping and hitting the ground; those few

113

seconds of doubt would not have occurred to her. Muriel would not have felt regret as she fell through the thin, winter air; she would have thought this is my act of judgement: this, my life coming to an end. *I am flying.*

Iris could see her now falling down, strangely slowly, over a cliff, her hair flying out around her, as if she was lying in water, her legs and arms outstretched like a star, open to finality, offering herself up to the slashing of her skin, the smashing of her bones, the rupture of her organs, the rapture of death.

Muriel's suicide note had been the flames that consumed the falconer's mews.

The funeral was a simple affair at the glen's chapel. The minister, a tall, upright man, gave a brief but moving service. Edward stared straight ahead, emotionless, while Louis didn't lift his eyes from the ground. But they stood together, united in their grief for their dead sister. The fragile Lady Melfort kept murmuring, 'My child, my child, my lost child,' and tears poured down her ravaged, broken face. Only Lord Melfort looked at the minister with an expression of unshakeability.

The estate workers stood at the back, their faces in shadow, watching the tableau in front of them. It was chilly in the chapel, and a small electric heater just below the minister's pulpit gave off some localized heat.

And, as the congregation stood there singing or whispering or listening to Psalm 23, they were united in this acceptance of the passing of life. Acknowledgement of their mortality joined aristocrat with worker. And also rendered each one alone, and equal. But the moment they set foot out of the chapel their roles reverted: one monied, the other not, and it was as if Muriel had never been.

As they were walking down the chapel path, Mrs Elliot turned to Iris.

'It's all your fault. Stirring up memories. You should never have come here.'

Before Iris could reply, the housekeeper had walked away. She watched as Mrs Elliot approached Coll, who was sobbing at the side of the path, and put her arm around him.

Chapter 22

After Muriel's funeral, Iris returned to her room where she collapsed on the bed. Her skin was hot, but inside she felt cold. Pain had become a centrifugal force and, unable to rest, she looked into the mirror and saw that all expression had drained from her face. She looked like a marble statue.

She sat in her chair for over an hour, waiting for warmth to return to her, and by the time she felt herself again, it was dark outside. The moon was a thin crescent. The night seemed to have been slit open, the moon glinting through the rent.

Iris leant her head on the arm of the chair, comforted by the pressure of the fabric against her forehead. At two o'clock she was awoken from her chair by the sound of tapping. The embers in the coal fire were still burning. Had someone been knocking on her door? She switched on the light, went over to the door, and opened it – but no-one was there; just the empty corridor.

The tapping began again – it was coming from the garden, just below her window, a repetitive, scratching noise on stone. She peered through the window but could only see the reflection of the interior of the room and her own stone face. She opened the window and looked out. A rustling sound was coming from the end of the garden, like the movement of a large animal. Iris stood at the window staring into the darkness. Then, suddenly, the rustling stopped and silence fell.

That night, Iris dreamt that Daphne was walking through the formal gardens toward the glen, as if in a trance. Daphne had her back to the castle, so she could not see the Melfort family looking down at her from various windows. Everyone but Muriel was watching her, each of them allowing Daphne to walk in the direction of the petrified forest as the beast cried out to her.

Muriel's death desolated Edward and Louis. They were like satellites around the sun of their pain. There was no diffuseness about the world of grief they now shared; everything in it was distinct. Their world was like the glen after it had rained and a bright light gave definition to the fields. And now the brothers had clear outlines too; their bodies shone with singularity.

Iris woke up one morning to find a letter had been slipped under her door. It was from Edward, simply asking her to meet him by the pool.

As she waited in the glade for him to appear, minutes turned to hours. The sun moved slowly over the trees while the white sky turned orange. She could not bear this waiting; it filled her with a shiftless dread. She began to feel petrified, as if turning into rock. She was beyond hope that he would appear but nonetheless she waited for him, waited for an appearance in the cold. Just as the sun was setting, her heart leapt – a man was appearing from the shadow of the glade.

She sprung to her feet. But as the shadows pulled away from his face to reveal his features, she saw that it wasn't Edward. His hair was too dark, his face too narrow. She was stymied. She felt foolish. Did he know that she had been waiting for so long, and for whom she had been waiting?

'I came to find you,' he said. 'I was told you'd be here.'

'By whom?'

'By Edward, of course. He's been detained. He thought you might still be waiting for him.'

Her legs felt heavy. Her body had stiffened. He reached out and took her hand. In the dusk it looked as if his eyes were burning with a white light. She felt scared, but also entranced.

'You're cold.'

117

He took off his threadbare jacket and put it round her shoulders – it smelled of seeds and bird feathers. They turned and walked back through the glade. They walked in silence for a while.

'So Edward told you where I would be?'

'Yes.'

'He told you I'd be waiting for him?'

'That's what I said, yes.'

'It was just a meeting. A friend's meeting.'

This time the falconer said nothing, but walked beside her. A bat flashed past their heads. It was almost nightfall. Not quite dark and not quite light. Why was she feeling so defensive? Why did she feel instinctively that she had to hide her desire for Edward? Because she knew that was what he wanted. And it was also what she wanted.

'He's done this before, you know,' the falconer said.

'Done what?'

'Left a lady waiting by the pool.'

She laughed nervously.

'It's what he likes to do. Keep people waiting,' the falconer said.

It was Daphne that Edward had kept waiting by the pool until dusk had fallen. He had kept her sister waiting as now he kept her. She felt out of breath, and she wasn't sure if it was because of the freezing night air or because of trepidation about what he might say next.

The lights of the falconer's cottage had appeared at the top of the rise. She felt overwhelmed by the questions she wanted to ask and could not, the information she needed but could not think of getting unless by subtle and disastrous ways.

And all her emotions were flooding to the surface of her, like blood to the surface of skin. Dense complicated feelings of rejection, fear, jealousy and desire. The falconer and Iris walked up the path to the road. Instead of turning right to the castle, wordlessly they turned left and walked towards the falconer's cottage. They went to bed. The sex was frenzied and animal and new. In the morning, while the falconer slept,

118

Iris took his blood-stained gauntlet from the table where his only remaining bird – the peregrine falcon – perched, and left.

Her jealousy of Edward's love for Daphne began to transfix her, the jealousy of Juno. Her jealousy was powerful; it filled up her chest, made her feel like a peacock strutting. And as she watched a peacock parade down the pathway of the garden, it seemed vibrant with the colours of envy.

With this jealousy, she didn't feel diminished: she felt huge and omniscient. She could sense the beautiful blue of her envy, with the black eye at the centre. She did not want to lose her hatred as the peacocks lost their feathers, leaving the feathers trailing forlornly on the path and their tails ragged. She wanted to keep all the feathers of her hatred intact – every one. Preen them, display them to admirers, arch them out for the sun to shimmer over their wondrous, oil-slick colours.

And now her sister was calling to her, calling to her through her black eye of jealousy. And where once the black eye seemed solid, now it seemed hollow, a hole through which other possibilities could shine through.

Daphne was walking towards her on the garden path. 'Please come over to the other side, Iris. I'm lonely here. You're unhappy on that side. Here, everything is softened by mist and dewdrops.'

She offered Iris her hand.

Chapter 23

Christmas was an unhappy, subdued affair without Muriel, and Lord Melfort seemed even more distant than usual. Iris spent the early weeks of the New Year making enquiries and advising Lord Melfort of the results. One evening, he summoned her into the library. She had never been to the library in the evening before. It seemed to be less of a place of work at night, and more a place of thoughts and dreams. In the dimly-lit room, the burning flames made the books look as if they were on fire.

Lord Melfort was sitting at his desk. The shadows gave him a certain nervous presence, as if he had now become haunted by a personality which had previously eluded him. He seemed less hidden, his emotions more naked in her presence than they had ever been before. He motioned her to sit down in one of the golden velvet armchairs that were usually reserved for his guests.

'There's something I would like you to consider doing for me, Iris.' He paused for a moment; she couldn't tell whether it was from difficulty in expressing what he had to say or from a dramatic need to highlight its importance. 'I rely very much on you and I want you to know how much I rely on you. I also know how you share my abhorrence for war.'

'It should always be the last resort,' she said simply. She stared at him. He had lost weight and his face had grown contorted with his anxiety.

'There are certain files that I have in my possession. We need a courier to carry these files to Germany. I ask this of you with great reluctance. I am a public figure and I cannot do this myself.'

'Why not give them to Herr Berger?'

'They tend to keep their eye on the German diplomats.'

She waited for him to continue.

'You must understand. It's for the good of our country. In the highly unlikely event of Germany considering war, the information in these files would make them think twice. And I trust you absolutely. Of course, you don't have to do what I ask. If you feel it is against your principles...'

Iris stood up. Her legs felt shaky. 'I need time to think this over.' she said.

'Of course,' he said, kindly.

As she shut the library door behind her, all she could hear was the great depth of silence from within.

Xavier buried his head in his hands. He had been so concerned for Louis to do the patriotic thing. He had lied to get Louis into the army, lied about his age. Father and son had been buoyed by euphoria, patriotism, naïveté. Louis had only been sixteen. He would never be able to forgive himself. He had sacrificed his eldest child. He wanted peace for his country now, at any price. He didn't want others to have to sacrifice the minds or the bodies of their sons, as he had done. He had been a misguided fool to think war was worth such easy sacrifices.

He had written Daphne's suicide note soon after they had watched Daphne leave the castle. He had then planted it in her bedside table. The same note that Louis now kept in his cabinet, to protect his father from the police. It had been important that the police concluded it was suicide. Any further investigations into the circumstances of Daphne's death might have led to an uncovering of his and Heinrich's plans.

Xavier had felt it was his own suicide note he was writing.

The next morning Iris knocked on Agnes' door.

'Come in.' Agnes turned from her desk when she saw Iris

enter, and beckoned her to her.

'So you've done what I've asked you? You've brought me the falconer's gauntlet?'

Iris took the bloodstained gauntlet with its tasselled loop of leather from under her coat, and gave it to her.

Agnes drew Iris into her gaze. It was like being sucked into a bottomless pool. It was only when she fixed Iris with that look that the extent of her power became apparent.

It was a magnetism that preyed on the weak and vulnerable, Iris thought. It would have no effect over the strong. It needed vulnerability to thrive; susceptibility was its lifeblood. Without another, weaker person's belief, her force was impotent. And Iris now accepted the depth of her own impressionability – *that she was no longer sure who she was.* And she knew that Agnes had realized it with a single glance, too.

'Now, what is it you want to know? One direct question in exchange for the gauntlet.'

Iris looked at her. 'Was Edward very much in love with her?' That Edward hadn't met her by the pool had shattered her lucid dreams. But she could still feel hope shifting under the blanket of reality, like a buried body under snow.

Agnes carefully put down the falconer's gauntlet on her desk and began to sort through various vials on the table. She looked very amused by the question, at the shift in emphasis from Iris' original quest.

'I was expecting a question about your sister's death. Or perhaps a question about the reality of the beast.' She gave Iris a sly look. 'Oh yes, Edward was very much in love with her. But you know, I'm not sure how long she would have remained in love with *him.*'

Spring came and the rain turned the waterfall to brown, stirred up with winter's bracken, earth and grit. As it cascaded over the rocks, the water sprayed the snowdrops growing at its edges. In the continuous rain, sheep and lambs cowered bedraggled under trees. But Iris could sense, under the relentless fall of the rain, that the earth was being quenched after the preceding dry weeks.

One late afternoon as she walked through the glen, Iris heard the howling again, a primeval sound coming from the direction of the petrified forest. It was beguiling. She crossed the bridge to the other side of the river and, entering the forest, began to walk to its centre.

She had almost reached the heart of the forest, the stone trees growing denser all around her, when she heard the heavy sound of a large animal crashing towards her through the trees. Desire turned to fear. Iris began to run, fast, panic-stricken. Jumping over stone branches on the ground, avoiding rabbit holes that could catch and twist her ankles, she became her velocity. As the animal chased her she could hear its brutish breathing and its paws thudding on the forest floor, smell its animal scent of flesh, sweat and acrid urine. After a while, she had no idea how long, the thudding behind her started to recede.

The beast curled up between the petrified roots of his tree, panting. He slowly shut his eyes and listened to the rustle of animals and the distant curlew. The ground, lined with pale stone dust, was comfortable under his weight. As the sun set, painting scarlet bands of silk across the bluey-green sky above the mountains, the creature's breathing became heavier and deeper until he finally fell asleep. He had smelt her fear.

Iris shut the door of her room in the castle behind her, fell into her chair and waited for her breathing to slow. She tried to light a fire with shaking hands, but the matches blew out one after another, until finally the kindling lit.

An hour or so later she drew a bath and pulled off her clothes, her undergarments stiff from her perspiration. She sank into the warm, lavender-scented water, leaning her head against the bath, feeling its cold iron on the back of her neck. What had disturbed her most was how the animal's cry had entranced her, how it had seemed to lure her towards itself.

It was far away now – whatever it had been – the animal had receded into the wood. It was skulking somewhere. She was safe now, in her bath of warm water, and she could relegate the animal to her dreams. But it was in her dreams that the reality of her life existed.

That night, Iris dreamt of Daphne stumbling into the petrified forest, bewitched by the beast's cry. Black lesions were covering her skin. The black marks on her body were like the dark patterns of the bark of a silver birch. She was walking to the centre of the wood. She lay down by the root of the stone tree and waited for her death to come to her.

In February, Heinrich Berger arrived in the glen again, and Iris instinctively felt that it was because of what Lord Melfort had asked her to do. Iris had still not decided whether to agree to his request. It was a momentous decision, and she had asked Lord Melfort to give her more time.

One day, Iris walked into the hallway and overheard Heinrich barking orders at a servant. His voice sounded completely different. His tone was violent rather than diffident, his German accent highly pronounced. The next morning, she saw Heinrich walk out of the castle and down the avenue towards the chapel. She followed him, saw him stand for a moment at Daphne's grave, and then enter the church.

She found him sitting at one of the pews, underneath the stained glass window that depicted the story of Isaac. He turned around when he heard her come in. His fair hair was immaculately oiled back, his features angular; everything about him had been completed, she thought. There was no room for other possibilities. Her heart felt cold.

'Are you here to pray for forgiveness?' Iris asked, sardonically.

He made a vague, contemptuous gesture towards the simple wooden cross on the communion table. 'In Germany, we no longer believe in these kind of Christian, womanly,

124

things. To us, religion is a dictatorship of morality. We worship nature instead. The forest. That is where the true gods live, courageously and intuitively.

'We do not ask for forgiveness. If we do our duty, we do not need to feel guilt.'

'And exactly what form does doing your duty take?'

Heinrich ignored her question. 'Xavier has told me that you are thinking of helping us.'

Iris nodded. Xavier was indeed Hitler's lure, she thought.

'You wouldn't want to lose Edward in another war, would you, Iris? Or risk him being wounded? He would be young enough to fight again. He might not be so lucky a second time.' Heinrich stopped for a moment, and then tried another approach. 'Louis has told me of your feelings of guilt over Daphne's death. What better way to make atonement? If you can prove to our Führer the strength of Britain's defences, you will rule out all *possibility* of war. Prevent the needless sacrifice of soldiers and innocent civilians' lives.'

'What about the needless sacrifice of Daphne's life? It was *you* Muriel heard speaking to Daphne on the night she died, wasn't it? Daphne was pleading for help. But you didn't try to stop her.'

'You must realize, Iris, that your sister had become convinced the beast was waiting for her. That he was calling for her to come into the forest. We all heard him.'

Terrible March winds fell, and the wind blew through the falconer's burnt mews, shaking its charred wooden remains. He had not touched his mews since the fire. Violent gusts shook his cottage's shutters as the walls shuddered beneath their strength. Like an angry spirit, the wind pushed between the gaps of the doors and the windows, as if trying to smash his home to pieces.

At the same time Iris, too, became reckless, as if the wind was infecting her with its unpredictable energy. She found herself soaking up its nervous rage, and the louder the squall became, the more she found it difficult to find her own peace. She became increasingly desperate, and diffuse, like the wind.

Iris knocked at the door of the falconer's cottage and came in with the force of the gale, rainwater running down her cheeks. Her hair was blown across her eyes, her face reddened from the blustering storm.

'What are you doing here?'

'Sometimes I hear the beast calling out to me. I'm sure the beast is following me.'

'You are sounding just like Daphne, before she died. Come in. Sit in front of the fire.' He looked at her gently.

'You knew she'd gone into the forest,' Iris said to his back as he put more wood on the fire. 'Living here, you would have heard her screams.'

The falconer looked out of his window and saw the birds flying in the sky. And he felt he were flying in the sky, spreading his wings, free-floating on the warmer undercurrents.

When he had first seen Daphne arrive in the glen, he hadn't known where to look. There was nowhere he had wanted to look except straight ahead. For without question or thought, he had been drawn to her; an inevitable drawing towards, as the evening draws in. This love came not from the body or the heart, but from a profound need in an indeterminate world. This meant that his will had been pure, and her being as white as the river's foam.

He had taught her how to fly the birds. He had watched as Daphne had seduced one brother then the next. And the obedience of his hawk seemed to mock him, seemed to say, look what you can do with this falcon, but you cannot to this wild, perverse woman who doesn't understand the bonds of love. He took one look at her and thought what graceful flights she could make, how she would be able to soar and swoop and react to his every command.

His desire for her petrified him like the trees of the forest. Her living breathing body turned his body to stone. And

126

every turn of the falcon, every flutter of its wing, every silent gaze seemed to be about what she could also do for him – but would not. And her wet hair reminded him of the falcon's wing and her white skin of the stone trees.

'The family had no other choice. Just as you've had no choice but to betray me to Agnes,' the falconer said.

'I always had the choice,' Iris replied.

Soon after Iris had returned to her room in the castle, there was a knock on the door and Edward entered. She was too frightened at the thought of what she might hear if she asked him about Daphne. They talked desultorily for a while, before Iris asked,

'What if your mother's right, Edward? And everyone else is wrong? That Hitler *is* intent on war? That Heinrich is deceiving you? That your attempt to stop another war is futile?'

Edward put his arm around her. 'Don't worry, my little cuckoo, God is on our side. I know we're right.' In the darkness, they retired to bed together. She heard him undress and felt him slip in beside her. She was grateful for any force that reminded her she was human. She felt his hot breath on her face as he kissed her. She kissed him back, passionately. The howling left her. She had the sensation, when she was making love to Edward, that it was too late to go back. But back to where, she didn't know.

Edward left soon afterwards. Lying there alone, she thought it all made sense – their separateness, their independence and their furtive touching. That their real lives were all happening in secret behind closed doors, beneath the veneer of their fearless exteriors.

In the glen that night Agnes cast her spell over the gauntlet, and the falconer took the shape of a falcon and flew into the sky.

The following morning, the transformed falcon drew a circle

in the sky high above, wheeling and waiting. The leaves of the oak trees below were luminous in the light spring breeze. The falcon was sharp-edged, its feathers cut at angles, a series of triangles, its beak strong and hooked. The falcon looked distinct but every beat of the countryside, every nuance of sound and whisper of light was part of what its life consisted of. The bird's motives were as pure and cruel as its flight.

From the point of view of the falcon the glen was a place of depth, a place of perspective. Everything was disparate; ferns, rocks, running streams and cavernous pools. The glen leapt up dramatically or sank down. There was the flat moor and there were the towering mountains. There was the bellowing of the rutting deer and the squeaking of the voles. Living creatures dug deep into the ground or soared up high.

Chapter 24

The glen was a sensual place; nature was made of flesh and bone. June came and the fox-gloves grew as high as her shoulders. Luscious purple rhododendrons, a rich man's flower, had spread into the wild. Honeysuckle was coming out, its sweet perfume filling the air. As her sister crossed over the field towards her, Iris for the first time noticed a pregnant swell to Daphne's belly.

'I thought perhaps you were Queen Mab in disguise,' Iris said to her. 'Did Agnes summon you up?'

The phantom just smiled.

'Daphne, why did you go into the wood?'

'I couldn't resist the beast calling out to me. Not like you. You were always stronger than me, Iris.'

'I'm sorry, Daphne, that I wasn't there to help you.'

Daphne put her arms around her, and Iris felt the strong pull of her presence before her sister vanished into the air. Iris was left with the dew on the grass and the swifts dancing in the sky.

'I'm sorry, Daphne,' Iris said to the empty landscape, 'that I didn't love you enough.'

Iris walked down the path towards the edge of the pool. She looked down at her reflection. She saw herself being sucked up into the water, finally becoming part of the natural world. She felt that she was falling deep into the pool, falling through its depths, that the pool was bottomless. As she fell, she saw that floating through the water were leaves and rocks and then flowers; roses and petunias and irises in pinks, purples and creams, just their blossoming heads against the dark black of the water. Then birds were flying through the

129

water, eagles, swallows, hawks, as if the pool had turned to sky and she kept flailing until everything turned to the black of the blackest deepest water.

As Iris walked down the narrow corridors to Edward's studio, she realized that her feelings for him had become a mixture of anguish and fear.

On seeing her enter, Edward pulled the damp cloth off the stand, and with a flourish revealed Iris' finished head. It stared back at her. Unlike the stare of Daphne's statue, Iris' gaze seemed to look straight through her creator. There was no desire for him in her eyes, only a look, as if a feeling had been sacrificed.

'Iris, the rainbow. The messenger of the gods,' he said.

Iris turned and looked at him with the same expression as her clay head. She had made up her mind to carry a message – not to Germany, but to the British authorities. A message of the Melforts' betrayal, of a collective sickness that had transformed Glen Almain into a corrupted dream. A collective sickness that had poisoned her sister's mind and body.

'I hear my father has asked you to be his courier,' Edward continued.

She realized that Edward had never loved her. He had used her for his own ends, so she would stay in the glen to help his father.

'Perhaps I'm not the kind of messenger he wants,' she said quietly. Tears began to pour down her face.

Edward understood her words immediately. 'You mean you would betray us to the British authorities? You mustn't betray us, Iris. Muriel knew nothing about it. Coll played no part. My father would be detained at his Majesty's pleasure, if not executed.'

'What about the pain you caused *my* family?' she asked through her tears. 'You and your family just watched as Daphne wandered towards the forest. *She was the mother of your unborn child.*'

130

'So you know, then, how much I had to sacrifice, don't you?'

How cold he sounded, she thought, how rational, but it concealed a kind of madness. She was still crying, unstoppable tears coursing down her face.

'Please stop crying, Iris. You're becoming quite hysterical.'

'It's you who've lost your mind,' she replied.

The seeds of the feathery grass had transformed the tips of the grass to silver. At the end of a heatwave, a softness had crept over the glen, rain threatened and a gentle humidity was seeping in.

At dawn, Iris crept out of her room and down the staircase out of the castle. No-one else was awake. A fox stood at the edge of the entrance to the avenue. The fox looked at Iris with its small, green eyes. The specificity of the fox. Every movement was precise. Framed by the bushes it looked almost comical, as if it was wearing on its head a green wig of leaves. Then suddenly it darted out, running across the garden, past the trimmed hedges and into the green shade of the old yew tree, where its red lithe body merged with the shadows.

Iris was pregnant with Edward's child. She had told no-one. She had known, even before the month had finished and there was no sign of blood. She felt different. Her skin felt more tactile, as if it was covered in silver glitter. It seemed to shimmer, not in a comfortable way, but as if she had been dipped in metal.

She shut her eyes and listened to the birds singing. Never had the sound seemed so bewitching. Music was the consolation of life.

Carrying her suitcase, Iris walked down the avenue of the castle and onto the road that wound its way down the glen. No-one had seen her go; no-one would be able to prevent her leaving. The far-off horizon was shining. Like the drawn-up curtain of a theatrical stage, a thick band of grey cloud hung above the background of a paler sky.

She looked around her. It would be the last time she would see the twisting, amber river, flecked by white where it crushed itself against the stones, the fragile birches, and the shadows of the surrounding mountains.

She passed the deserted falconer's cottage, and continued down the road towards the station. The birdsong echoed the dawning sky – an orchestration of light breaking.

The End

Acknowledgements

With gratitude to Sharon Blackie, David Knowles, Jonny Geller, Doug Kean, Matt Thompson, Professor Alan Thompson, Janey Jones, Geraldine Aramanda, Auchingarrich Falconry Centre and Stephen Lloyd.

Works cited:

p 19	*The Encyclopaedia of Falconry* by Adrian Walker
p 47 & 82	*The Age of Fable* by Thomas Bullfinch
p 67	*Kubla Khan* by Samuel Taylor Coleridge
p 76	*The Lady of Shalott* by Alfred Tennyson

Fiction from Two Ravens Press

Love Letters from my Death-bed: by Cynthia Rogerson
£8.99. ISBN 978-1-906120-00-9. Published April 2007

Nightingale: by Peter Dorward
£9.99. ISBN 978-1-906120-09-2. Published September 2007

Parties: by Tom Lappin
£9.99. ISBN 978-1-906120-11-5. Published October 2007

Prince Rupert's Teardrop: by Lisa Glass
£9.99. ISBN 978-1-906120-15-3. Published November 2007

The Most Glorified Strip of Bunting: by John McGill
£9.99. ISBN 978-1-906120-12-2. Published November 2007

One True Void: by Dexter Petley
£8.99. ISBN 978-1-906120-13-9. Published January 2008

Auschwitz: by Angela Morgan Cutler
£9.99. ISBN 978-1-906120-18-4. Published February 2008

The Long Delirious Burning Blue: by Sharon Blackie
£8.99. ISBN 978-1-906120-17-7. Published February 2008

The Last Bear: by Mandy Haggith
£8.99. ISBN 978-1-906120-16-0. Published March 2008

Double or Nothing: by Raymond Federman
£9.99. ISBN 978-1-906120-20-7. Published March 2008

The Credit Draper: by J. David Simons
£9.99. ISBN 978-1-906120-25-2. Published May 2008

Vanessa and Virginia: by Susan Sellers
£8.99. ISBN 978-1-906120-27-6. Published June 2008

Short Fiction & Anthologies

Highland Views: by David Ross
£7.99. ISBN 978-1-906120-05-4. Published April 2007

Riptide: New Writing from the Highlands & Islands: Sharon Blackie & David Knowles (eds)
£8.99. ISBN 978-1-906120-02-3. Published April 2007

Types of Everlasting Rest: by Clio Gray
£8.99. ISBN 978-1-906120-04-7. Published July 2007

The Perfect Loaf: by Angus Dunn
£8.99. ISBN 978-1-906120-10-8. Published February 2008

Cleave: New Writing by Women in Scotland. Edited by Sharon Blackie
£8.99. ISBN 978-1-906120-28-3. Published June 2008

Poetry

Castings: by Mandy Haggith
£8.99. ISBN 978-1-906120-01-6. Published February 2007

Leaving the Nest: by Dorothy Baird
£8.99. ISBN 978-1-906120-06-1. Published July 2007

The Zig Zag Woman: by Maggie Sawkins
£8.99. ISBN 978-1-906120-08-5. Published September 2007

In a Room Darkened: by Kevin Williamson
£8.99. ISBN 978-1-906120-07-8. Published October 2007

Running with a Snow Leopard: by Pamela Beasant
£8.99. ISBN 978-1-906120-14-6. Published January 2008

In the Hanging Valley: by Yvonne Gray
£8.99. ISBN 978-1-906120-19-1. Published March 2008

The Atlantic Forest: by George Gunn
£8.99. ISBN 978-1-906120-26-9. Published April 2008

Butterfly Bones: by Larry Butler
£8.99. ISBN 978-1-906120-24-5. Published May 2008

For more information on these and other titles, and for news, reviews, articles, extracts and author interviews, see our website.
All titles are available direct from the publisher, postage & packing-free, at
www.tworavenspress.com
or from any good bookshop.